Acknowledgements

I acknowledge, with grateful thanks, all whose contributions have proved to be invaluable to me in my efforts to deliver a story to give the reader a flavour of what life was like for the poor in Glasgow and Scotland in the latter half of the nineteenth century. In particular, thanks to my son, John, who suggested the idea for the book; to the other members of my family whose feedback kept me and the story on course; to Terry Murray for his constant encouragement; to the staff of the Local Studies Discovery Room in Airdrie Library – Allan Mackenzie for his constant willingness to help and Monica Ferguson whose offer to proof-read the final draft was gratefully accepted. I would also like to give a special mention to my father, "Big Jackie", whose anecdotes and reminiscences have contributed much to the colour of the characters and events contained within the book.

Sam Gracey

3

Dedication

To Zoe Emma Freer

When good St Mungo preached and prayed,
By moor and glen and forest glade,
He reached a knoll with a burn beside,
That looked on a valley green and wide.
The good St Mungo smiled and said:
"No prospect could be finer,
We'll build our cell by this crystal well,
On the banks of the Molendinar".
Rev. Robert Macomish

Chapter One

The Dear Green Place

Where I lived wasn't the worst slum in the world. The worst slum in the world would still have been a better place to live than the Wynds of Glasgow in the 1800s. But it was there that I was born and where I spent the first few years of my life, along with thousands of the poorest and most miserable wretches who had the misfortune to be cast up on the wharves of the Empire's Second City. Yet, to listen to the older folks, including my own parents and grandparents, even this was preferable to what they had left behind when they fled the blighted potato fields and the subsequent politically-permitted famine in Ireland or the various persecutions being carried out from Russia all the way to the Atlantic Ocean.

Most, but not all, of the inhabitants of the Wynds were Irish-born or first generation Scots of Irish stock. There were also indigenous Scots, Jews, Russians and Armenians amongst a real mish-mash of European detritus. However, at that time, to me it just seemed like the norm and it was only in later years when I had been around a bit, that I appreciated just how bad conditions had been there.

My father, mother and I lived at number 110 Old Wynd, where I was born. Our home consisted of one room with one window which overlooked a small courtyard. There was an alcove which was filled with a bed (a box-bed it was called) and all three of us slept in this bed. We had an old, stained sink but no water tap and a cupboard underneath, another small cupboard against a wall, a built-in range-type fire which was our sole source of heating and cooking, two old wooden straight-backed chairs, a table and my father's chair, which I always thought of whenever the priest at the Mass told the story of the ten lepers. I imagined it to be covered in sores and erupting pus but, in reality, it had just seen better days and was showing more of its insides than it hid. Our water had to be obtained from a tap on the outside wall downstairs. This water, which was sourced from the polluted water of the river Clyde was always a shade of brown, never clear, and my mother had to boil this water before we could drink it. The floor of the house was made of wooden floorboards. Over the years most of the floor had seen a lot of small repairs but it was still in a very poor condition. Most of the boards had gaps of varying widths between them and these gaps provided shelter for all sorts of insects, especially cockroaches. Most of the time, we didn't worry about these insects, apart from making sure that we cleaned them up after crushing them underfoot. As a result, the floor was covered with small blotches of various colours, depending on what kind of insect had been killed. My mother, however, had a phobia about earwigs and would actually run away when she saw one, so it would be left to my father to kill it, as she had made me as scared as herself with all her talk of how earwigs would crawl into your ears and burrow into your brain! For years afterward I couldn't see an earwig without experiencing a shudder of fear.

Apart from the window, the only other source of light was a gas mantle, but a lot of the time there was no gas and we had to use candles. The only decorations in the house were two little china ornaments that my Granny Lizzie had given to my parents as a wedding present, a crucifix and a faded colour image of the Sacred Heart.

Everybody I knew lived in the same kind of house. In some of the houses there could be as many as seven or eight people. Those who didn't sleep in the box bed would sleep on a mattress which was pulled out from below the bed. My mother had three children, two girls and me. One sister, who had been called Lizzie after my mother's mother, Granny Lizzie, had been born before me but she had died of consumption when I was a baby. My other sister, called Mary Ann, after my mother, had died three days after she was born. I can remember all the people coming to our house and saying the Rosary with Father McHugh then my father carried a small box down the stairs and put it on my Uncle Willie's handcart. Then all the people that were there, walked

7

behind the handcart down the Wynd and into Bridgegate. They walked along Bridgegate and then along Clyde Street until they reached St Andrew's chapel. By the time everybody reached the chapel they were all soaked, as the rain of the last two days had continued into that morning. I don't remember much about the Mass and, after it was over, the men took the box back out of the chapel. All the women were crying except my mother, who squeezed my hand as she led me out. Father McHugh and the men set off again with the box on the handcart and headed towards the Green, but all the women and children went back to the Wynd. It was only in later years that I found out that they had walked the three miles to the graveyard where Mary Ann was buried.

My grandmother, aunts and some of the neighbours went back to the house with my mother, but I stayed outside playing in the rain with my pals. It was getting dark by the time my father came home with my uncle Willie. They were both steaming drunk! My mother and I were already in bed pretending to be asleep, as my father was usually in a bad mood when he was drunk and would do a lot of shouting and bawling. Sometimes, if my mother was arguing with him, he would start hitting her until she collapsed to the floor, crying.

Uncle Willie sat down on my father's chair and fell asleep. My father got into the bed and, within a few minutes, he too was sleeping. I lay on the inside, facing my mother. As I was drifting off, I could feel her shaking and I felt the wetness of her silent tears on my own face.

In those days there were lots of funerals in the Wynds, mostly of children, but that was one of only two where I can remember my mother crying. Even when my father died later, I didn't see her cry.

To get to our house we had to climb an outside staircase which, for most of the year, was covered in all manner of substances from moss to stuff blown in from the surrounding area. All sorts of shit was carried in on the wind from the slaughterhouse, the fish market, the clothes markets and surrounding industries. The big problem was that the south entrances to the Wynds faced towards the river and the prevailing wind. In the case of Old and Back Wynds, the northern entrances were little more than covered alleyways so, there being nowhere for this shit to go, it stayed where it landed. Although Glasgow had street cleaners and even carts that carried massive barrels of water that was sprayed on the streets to clean them even more, none of these services were to be found in the Wynds or other such areas of the city. What fell or was dropped on the ground, stayed on the ground. What made the whole situation worse was the narrowness of the Wynds. At some points the gap between the two sides was as little as twelve feet but, even at its widest point, Old Wynd was never more than twenty feet across, if that. It was almost as easy to know the business of the neighbours opposite as it was of those who lived in the same building. What this also meant, of course, was that disease spread rapidly through the population and illnesses like smallpox, typhus, measles, scarlet fever and tuberculosis, amongst others, wreaked havoc. The worst example of this was the great cholera outbreak which occurred before I was born. At the height of the outbreak, thousands had died and were buried in mass graves. I have no doubt that our house would, most probably, have been lived in by victims of such diseases. Needless to say, there would have been no effort made to clean these hovels before the installation of fresh tenants.

As well as sticking to the stairs, all the stuff blown in by the wind also stuck to the buildings and, through time, acted as a base for moss and other plants to grow. When it rained, the water poured off the edges of the roofs and down the walls and this helped to feed the plants. If you stood in the street and looked up, it seemed as if all the buildings had been draped with green curtains by some demented decorator!

We also had our home-grown contributions to make. Like everyone else in the Wynds, we used a bucket as a toilet and as a rubbish bin. If it was only piss in the bucket then it was just emptied over the railing into the open gutter which ran down the centre of the street. Anything else was carted downstairs, through the close into the courtyard and deposited on the pile of rubbish, including human and horse shit, which lay in the middle of the yard. It took some time for me to understand the reason why this pile always seemed to stay more or less the same size despite the numerous contributions which were made on a daily basis. Rats! Lots and lots and lots of big, fat, filthy and fearless rats. Over in Back Wynd there was an old ground floor house that nobody lived in. It had no windows and people would just throw all their rubbish through the gaps and into the room. The old man who lived upstairs was employed by the landlords to load this rubbish on a handcart and take it away. For this he received a small amount of money and lived rent-free. This service was not provided through the landlords' altruism but rather to avoid their premises being condemned and their rental income being cut off.

Barney Flanagan, a carter, lived below us and kept his horse in the yard. At night, he took the horse into the house so that nobody could steal it. At any one time there could be up to four horses in residence around the yard. For a time, James Dunn at number 96 used to walk his horse up the stairs to his house but the landlord heard about it and kicked James out.

I suppose, like most of the people there, I was used to living in these conditions but in the summer months it became like hell for even the hardiest. As the temperature rose and the river level dropped, the usual foul air was made a thousand times worse by the smells carried from the sewer outfall at the bottom of Market Lane. As I later found out, this was in fact the mouth of the famous Molendinar Burn - the one-time crystal well beside which St Mungo had supposedly founded Glasgow. Over the years it had become little more than a giant sewer for the inhabitants and the industries along its course.

Chapter Two

The Laughing Goose

It may be hard to believe, but we were actually better off than a lot of people in the Wynds. We had a room to live in - such as it was. At the bottom end of the Wynds, the buildings were in such a bad condition that the owners were not allowed to charge rent for them. They were occupied by squatters of both sexes and all ages. From what I overheard of adult conversations, it seems that these squatters were mostly thieves and prostitutes. Although I had no idea what prostitutes were, I knew better than to ask, as that would have indicated that I had been listening when I was expected to be deaf as well as invisible.

Every now and again a detachment of Peelers armed with clubs and rifles would mount a raid into these hovels and, after a pitched battle, drag some people away. The rest would scatter through the closes into the yards and into the neighbouring streets and alleys.

It was during one of these raids that I first saw Goose Lavery as he was fleeing up the Wynd. I was standing at the railing watching the raid when I noticed him. He looked a little bit older than me and I was intrigued by the fact that he was laughing fit to burst. I shouted and gestured to him to come up the stairs. He hesitated briefly, shrugged and ran up the stairs and into the house still laughing like a maniac.

My mother, who was sitting at the table peeling potatoes, let out a scream and threw a spud at him.

"Mammy, it's all right he's my pal. I told him to come in," I shouted.

"Well why is he charging in like a wild bull and what is he laughing at?" she demanded.

"Sorry missus. I was running away from the Peelers. I didn't mean to frighten you" said Goose in a conciliatory manner, the laugh now reduced to a broad grin.

My mother had inherited that trait of distrust of the forces of the law which was so prevalent amongst the poor, particularly the Irish poor. However, she was even less trusting of someone who was on the run from those forces, until she found out why.

"So why are the Peelers after you, then?" she demanded to know.

"Wrong place at the right time, missus," Goose replied. "My da owed three shillings to Peter Wasson and sent me to give him the money."

Peter Wasson was the local moneylender who lived near the middle of Old Wynd. His house was reached through a close and across a yard next to the Free Church Mission. He would sit at a table in the yard and lend out money as well as take in payments.

"I had just paid him when people came swarming through the close like rats and scattered across the yard running from the Peelers. Wasson and his table were knocked over in the rush. I think he was knocked out, as his eyes were shut. When the Peelers came through the close I ran as well, but not before I got this," he continued and he showed us a small leather pouch which I hadn't noticed before.

He emptied the pouch onto the table. My mother gave a gasp and held both hands to her mouth. I doubted if she had ever seen so much money in one place before – I certainly hadn't and I very much doubt if Goose had either.

"How much do you think there is?" he asked. He was asking the wrong people. I was only seven at the time and could barely count beyond ten. I don't think my mother was much better. All I knew was that there were lots of silver coins amongst the coppers.

"Listen, son, if you get caught with that by Peter Wasson or his cronies you'll get murdered. You'd best be off back home before they start looking for his money" my mother warned him. "What's your name and where do you live," my mother asked.

"Isaac Lavery, but everybody calls me Goose and I live round in the Saltmarket" he replied. My mother got up from the chair, wrapped her shawl round her shoulders, took both of us by the hand and led us outside.

We went downstairs and up the Wynd into the bustle of the Trongate. We made our way along the Trongate and round into the Saltmarket. When we got to number 38, Goose said "We live through here."

My mother let go of his hand and ushered him through the close.

"Straight home now!" she ordered.

"Thanks missus," he replied and ran through the close.

"Willie," she said as we made our way home, "don't say anything about this to anybody, not even to your da. If he finds out he'll not be able to hold his peace when he gets a drink in him."

"Right, mammy" I replied knowing full well that she was dead right.

All during that night and for the two nights after, the Wynd echoed to shouts and screams of pain as Wasson and his gang beat and tortured their way through the squatters trying to track down the missing money.

On the fourth night, Wasson made the mistake of attacking a big Yorkshire sailor who was "visiting" one of the squatter women. Nobody knows whether the sailor was more annoyed about being attacked, or about being interrupted, but the upshot was that Wasson found himself with a stiletto knife hilt-deep in his left ear. That was the end of Wasson and of the treasure hunt.

It was two days before anyone did anything about the body but when it started to stink it was dumped at the door of the Free Church. By the time the Peelers arrived and started asking questions, the sailor was long gone. To be truthful, even if he had still been around, they wouldn't have caught him, as nobody told the Peelers anything. Although some would have co-operated if there was a reward involved, there wasn't anyone who cared enough about Wasson to offer as much as two pennies for information about his killer.

The Wynds had their own justice system. You didn't steal from your neighbour, as they probably had less than you. If disputes could not be settled peacefully, then fist fights were perfectly acceptable, but no liberties were to be taken. If a man, or a woman for that matter, went down and did not attempt to get back up then the fight was over. Under no circumstances did you co-operate with the Peelers. Break any of these unwritten rules and the consequences could be severe. Even so, it was not unknown for there to be the odd informer in our midst.

By far the most extreme example of Wynds justice lives in my memory to this day. At the time, I did not understand what "interfering with a wean" was, but I was sitting with my mother one Friday night, waiting for my father to come home from work via the Anchor Tavern, when we heard the sound of a woman screaming from across the street.

When we got to the door we could see Mary McGhee at her door just down the street from us. She had hold of a man by the hair and was beating him with a pot. She kept shouting that she had come home and had found him interfering with wee Mary Kate, who was a couple of years older than me, I think. I recognized the man as Mrs McGhee's brother who had lived with her since her husband had died in the Iron Works. (It was only later that I found out that he wasn't her brother.)

Within a minute, a lot of men came out of the Anchor Tavern and dragged him downstairs. From every window and doorway looking into the street, including ours, shawl-wrapped women were screaming at the men. "Murder the dirty bastard!",

"Kill him!" and a lot of other stuff about balls and pricks that I didn't understand. (Years later, I would come across engraved representations of the revolutionary executions carried out in Paris and would be instantly reminded of that evening.)

The men sat Mrs McGhee's "brother" on the bottom step of the stairway to her house. Three men were behind him. One held his head while the others held an arm each. Two other men, one of whom was my own father, held his legs straight out in front of him. From the close to the right of the stairway, big Mr Fogarty, who lived at number 114 and another even bigger man, whom I didn't know, came out carrying between them a big stone with a ring on it that was used as a hitching post.

They struggled over to the seated man and very deliberately dropped the heavy stone post straight across his knees. Strangely, while the crack of breaking bones could be clearly heard, it seemed like ages before the screams of the crippled man drowned out the shouts and cheers and jeers coming from all parts of the street. The men lifted the stone and two of them grabbed his arms, dragged him to the top of the Wynd and dumped him on the pavement on the Trongate.

All the men then returned to the Anchor. My mother sent me inside while she stayed outside talking to the neighbours. From what I could gather, the general opinion was that the man had got off lightly and that, if he ever showed his face again, assuming that he would ever walk again, he could expect a lot worse though, at that time, I could not imagine what could have been worse than what had just happened.

17

Chapter Three

Pennies and Heaven

A couple of weeks after the Wasson carry-on I was sitting with my mother in front of the fire trying to keep warm as the rain was battering down outside. As it was a Saturday, my mother was sitting knitting while she waited for two big pots of water to come to the boil to put into the tin bath that my father would use when he came back from his work at the Saracen Iron Works. He would usually come home about half past five, have his supper, his bath and then go out to the Anchor or some other pub. When he was finished with the bath, I would get in and my mother would wash me then dry me with the same towel that my father had used. If the weather was dry my mother would send me outside while she used the bath, but if it was raining she would put me on the bed and pull the bed curtains closed.

There was a knock on the door and when my mother opened it, there was Goose Lavery with a big box in his hands.

"Hello, missus," he said, "is it all right if I come in?"

My mother told him to come in and he put the box on the table.

"My ma sent this round to you to thank you for looking after me and taking me home," he said.

"Sure, that was no bother at all," my mother replied. "I'm sure your ma would have done the same for my wee Willie if it had been the other way round." Nevertheless, she opened the box and let out a small squeal of delight when she looked inside. I walked over

18

to her side and had a look as well, as she started taking things out. There was a loaf of bread, a block of cheese, two pats of butter, six apples, a paper bag with some eggs in it, a bottle of ginger beer and a red ribbon.

"Ah, son," she said to Goose, "she didn't have to do that but please tell her thanks very much."

"No bother, missus," replied Goose. "Is it all right for Willie to come out and play?" My mother looked out of the window, saw that the rain had stopped and said that I could go out, but that I had to come in when my father came home.

We went outside and down the stairs to the street, but it started to rain again so we ran up to the alley at the top of the Wynd. When we got there, Goose put his hand in his jacket pocket and brought out two sticks of barley sugar and handed one to me.

"There you go wee man," he said. I liked barley sugar but I didn't get it very often. We sat down with our backs against the alley wall and started sucking on the sticks. You could bite on the sticks and chew them but they lasted longer if you sucked them.

After a few minutes of silence, I asked Goose why he was called Goose when his real name was Isaac.

"Have you heard the story of Jack and the Beanstalk?" he asked. As it was one of the stories that my grandfather told me regularly, I jumped up and started stamping around in an exaggerated way growling "fee fi fo fum". Goose burst out laughing and said "Aye, that's the one. Well, you remember that the giant had a goose which laid golden eggs?"

"Don't tell me you lay golden eggs as well" I interrupted.

"No, ya wee eejit. When I'm out with my ma and da, we go round the doors of the big fancy houses asking the people in them if they've got anything they don't want. Because I usually get most of the good stuff handed to me, my da says that I'm like the goose that laid the golden eggs, so everybody calls me Goose. To tell you the truth, I prefer it because when I tell people that my name is Isaac they think I'm a yid."

"What's a yid?" I asked.

"What! You don't know what a yid is?" he exclaimed. When I shook my head in reply he told me that a yid was another name for a Jew.

"You know what a Jew is?" he asked.

"Aye. They're the ones that killed Jesus." I replied.

"That's right and you don't want people to think you're one of them, do you?" Again, I simply shook my head as I had started sucking on my barley sugar again.

After another couple of minutes of silence, I asked Goose what his mother and father did with the stuff they collected.

"Usually, they take it down to the Bazaar to sell, but sometimes they sell it down Market Lane."

I had been down to the Bazaar with my mother a few times and had found it to be a wondrous place. There was plenty of fancy stuff for people to buy but my mother had never bought anything when I was with her. I think she just enjoyed going down to see all the different people buying and selling all sorts of stuff that I had never seen before. One time she had taken me down and I cowered in fear when I saw a black man for the first time. I hid behind my mother but she brought me round in front of her and told me not to be scared as he was the same as us but that God had left him in the oven too long.

As I related this story to Goose, he nearly choked on his barley sugar.

"Left in the oven too long? Ha! That's a good one," he laughed. I laughed as well, but I didn't know what was funny as I really believed that what my mother had told me was the truth of the matter.

"I've seen hundreds of black men and Indians and chinks down the docks." Goose said. I knew where the docks were because when we went to chapel, we could see all the ships along the river, but I had never been up close to them. I told Goose this and he said that he would take me down sometime.

"No, my ma will never let me go away down there. I'm not allowed to leave the Wynd unless I'm going to my granda's in Bridgegate or my other granda's in Back Wynd,"

"I'll ask my ma to ask your ma if you can come down with us some time when we're going down there."

"What do you go down there for?" I asked.

"We go round the pubs selling stuff to the sailors. When they get drunk they will buy anything off you and my da says that they can't count their change right. But he always has to give the owner a shilling so that we can sell our stuff in his pub." I told him that I would love to do that but I wasn't sure that my mother would let me go.

"I can go anywhere I want because I'm nearly ten" boasted Goose. I was astonished because he was only slightly taller than me and I was only approaching my eighth birthday.

"How come you're not bigger then?" I asked, not totally convinced that he was telling me the truth.

"My ma says that good things come in small quantities," he laughed. "She told me that I had been in a hurry to be born because Christmas was coming and I didn't want to miss it."

I understood why he would have been in a hurry because I liked Christmas too. While my father had to go to work, my mother would take me down to the chapel to see the baby Jesus in the stable. Then, after the Mass, Father McHugh or one of the other priests would hand out sweets or apples to all the children. I preferred the sweets because the apples were hard and didn't taste very good.

I asked Goose if he preferred the sweets or the apples.

"We don't go to chapel anymore," he replied. I was confused because it seemed that everybody I knew went to chapel.

"Are you a Protestant or a pagan?" I asked since the priests told us that only Protestants and pagans didn't go to chapel. I was fearful that my new pal was going to go to hell when he died.

"No, I'm a Catholic, the same as you," said Goose. "But when I was nine, we were up in a place called Fife and my wee sister was really sick after she was born. My da went to the priest and asked him to come and baptise her in case she died. The priest told him to go and bring her back with him as he couldn't be going out in the snow, which had fallen really early that year. My da came and got her but when he got back to the priest's house she was dead. The priest told my da that it was too late and that her soul had gone to Limbo where all babies' souls go if they die without being baptised. My da came back, got a spade and went out and buried her in a field after clearing the snow away. When my ma protested that she had to be buried in a proper grave my da said that it didn't matter and that the Catholic Church and all their lazy, bastarding priests could go and take a fuck to themselves from now on. So, since then, we don't go to chapel anymore."

I listened, totally amazed that somebody could talk about the Church and the priests like that. My limited experience led me to believe that just about everyone lived in fear of upsetting the priest because that would be the same as upsetting God. However, realising that it would probably be better not to tell Goose that he and his family would all be going to hell, I kept my mouth shut.

Just then, a man staggered into the alley from the Trongate. He put his left forearm against the wall, leant his head on his arm, unbuttoned his trousers, took out his penis and started pissing against the wall. While he was pissing he started singing at the top of his voice

"The pale moon was rising above the green mountains, the sun was declining beneath…"

Before he could finish the line, he leant too far to his right, swivelled on his right foot, fell against the wall, banged the back of his head and slowly slipped to the ground until he was in a sitting position with his penis still hanging out.

"Come on," said Goose and he ran up to the sitting figure. He took hold of the man's shoulders and pulled him over till he was lying down then he started going through his pockets. I stood watching, open-mouthed. Goose got up, showed me a shilling and some coppers and told me to follow him. We ran down past my house and into the yard at the back. Goose handed me the coppers and told me that they were my share.

"But, Goose, that's stealing and my ma will want to know where I got the money from," I protested.

"Look, Willie. That drunken bastard would only have spent the money on more drink. He won't even know what happened when he wakes up. Besides, just think what you'd be able to buy in the Bazaar if you had some money. Take it and hide it where your ma won't find it."

My reluctance didn't last long as I imagined myself buying all sorts of exotic items, or even some more barley sugar.

As we came out of the yard back into the Wynd, my mother came out onto the landing and shouted to me to come in for my supper as my father was home. Goose told me that he would have to get home too, but that he would come back round tomorrow and he headed off down towards Bridgegate. As I made my way up the stairs, I stopped on the fourth step and pulled a loose stone out of the wall, put my coppers in the space and replaced the stone. This was quite an easy process; much of the mortar between the stones had crumbled and several of the stones were loose. Having hidden my first ill-gotten gains, I carried on up the stairs and into the house.

Chapter Four

The Best Tunes

The following morning, my mother got me up to get ready for chapel. She gave me a bit of bread and cheese for my breakfast along with some tea. My mother and father only had a cup of tea because they would be receiving Holy Communion and they weren't allowed to eat anything for three hours before, although they could drink something as long as it was an hour before. I knew that I would soon be making my First Holy Communion in May and that I wouldn't be able to eat anything then either. However, what was most worrying for me was the fact that I would be making my First Confession before my First Communion and I knew that I would have to tell the priest about the money that Goose and I had stolen.

We walked down to the chapel with a lot of other people. The men, who all seemed to be dressed in the same black suits, walked together leaving the women with all the children. When we entered the chapel, all the children went down towards the front where the nuns were. The women sat behind the children and the men sat right at the back.

When the priest, whom I didn't know, came out onto the altar with four altar boys, the nuns started singing a hymn that we had learned at school and we all joined in. When the hymn was finished, the priest and the altar boys said all the usual stuff in Latin. After about ten minutes, the priest turned round and walked over to the pulpit and read out something about, what sounded to me, at that time, like a "pissel from St Paul". After that, he said some more stuff in Latin then read out a Gospel story about Jesus and a Roman soldier and his servant.

Then, we all sat down and the priest started to talk about how it was a disgrace that a Roman seemed to believe more in Jesus than some of the people who had been baptised as Catholics, but who behaved more like pagans. In particular, he had aimed his criticism at those men who would go out and get drunk saying that getting drunk was a mortal sin and that they would burn in the fires of hell. As he said this he was shouting and banging his hand down on the pulpit. No wonder the men all sat at the back. It turned out that this was a mission priest who came every year and always said the same thing about drinking. For my part, I was relieved because, according to my twisted logic or wishful thinking, Goose and I had stopped a man from committing another mortal sin by taking his money that he was only going to spend on drink. There would be no need to bother the priest at confession after all.

The priest's words didn't seem to bother the men too much either because, when it was time for Holy Communion, every one of them knelt at the altar rail and received the host. After the Mass was finished, everybody walked back to the Wynd. Most of the men broke into groups and stood around smoking and laughing and joking. I went home with my mother and she took off my Sunday clothes and put my old stuff on. Then she sent me out to play while she started peeling spuds for the dinner.

I went outside and started playing with some of the other children. For a change, the sun was shining and we spent a couple of hours playing hide and seek. It was only later on, as I passed my hiding place on the stairs when going for my dinner, that I realised that Goose hadn't come round like he had said he would.

My mother had made a pot of stew with turnip and carrots and had put it out on three plates with some spuds. My father got the biggest plate and he sat in his chair and leaned over to the table to eat his, whilst my mother and I sat on the wooden chairs. When we had finished the spuds and stew, we used some bread to soak up the juice that was left.

"Is the wee fellow going out to play again, Mary?" my father asked. My mother gave a sigh and said that I was. She gave me one of the apples that Goose had brought and sent me outside. As I was walking down the stairs munching on the apple, I heard the key turning in the lock behind me. It was some years later before I understood why the door was sometimes locked behind me when I went out.

There was nobody about that I wanted to play with, so I sat on the bottom step eating my apple and all the time thinking about the money I had hidden in the wall. I had just finished my apple and thrown the core into the street when I heard Goose's voice shout "All right there, Willie boy?" I looked across and saw him standing at the close beside Mary McGhee's house. I walked over to him.

"I thought you weren't coming," I said.

"My ma sent me up to Weaver Street with a message for my auntie Alice and I stayed there for my dinner so I only got back a wee while ago."

"Weaver Street? Where's that?" I asked.

"It's away up beside the Royal Infirmary."

"Oh right," I said not having a clue *what* the Royal Infirmary was never mind *where* it was.

Suddenly, Goose grabbed my arm and pointed down the street at a small crowd, led by dark figure, which was making its way up the Wynd. I recognised the figure as being the mission priest from the chapel that morning and that he was being accompanied by some of the nuns from the school. The nuns were clapping their hands and singing while the priest was shouting at the top of his voice about how God and Jesus loved us all and that we would all go to hell if we didn't love them back.

"Fuck this," said Goose and he dragged me through the close into the yard at the back. "Come on wee man," he shouted as he ran through into another yard. I followed him through the other yard and through a close till we reached the New Wynd. The New Wynd was different from the other Wynds. Although it was just as narrow as the others, it had a full street opening onto the Trongate. I had never been this far up, as I was used to crossing further down when I was going to my grandfather's house in Back Wynd. I knew there was a pub at the top because I had passed it when I was in the Trongate with my mother. In fact, we had passed it that time when my mother was taking Goose home.

"Fucking hymns," Goose spat. "Do you want to hear some real music, Willie?" When I nodded my head in reply he said "Good. Come on then" and started walking up the street. When we reached the top, I could hear somebody singing from inside the building. Goose walked out onto the Trongate and I followed. We walked a short distance and then went through an alley into the top of Back Wynd. As we came through the alley, Goose turned into a doorway. There were two doors and one was slightly open. Goose held his finger to his mouth for me to keep quiet and inched inside the open door. He had a look then beckoned for me to follow.

Inside, there was a flight of stairs and we crept up them. While climbing the stairs, I could hear a woman singing followed by what seemed like hundreds of people joining in. When we got near the top of the stairs I saw a man wearing dark trousers, a shiny yellow waistcoat and a bowler hat. He had his back to us and was lustily joining in with the singing. Goose nodded to me to follow and we crept past him to a further flight of stairs.

When we got to the top, he opened a door and I followed him through. What I saw almost took my breath away. We were high up, looking down at the figure of a woman standing on a stage. In front of her was a band playing and all the people down at the bottom, as well as all those around us, were singing along while moving their heads from side to side in time with the music. I had never seen so many people in one place before, not even when the chapel was full.

When the woman had finished, a man came on and started to tell jokes. I didn't understand a lot of them so I just laughed when everyone else did. After the comic, another man came on to sing, but he had to stop because everybody was booing and throwing things at him.

Another woman came on and sang some songs, but nobody joined in because she was singing so high, but she must have been good because everybody clapped after she finished. After the woman, came a man who was juggling clubs, but he kept dropping them and he was booed as well. It seemed that every five minutes somebody different came on; singers, men telling jokes, a man who did magic tricks. There was even a pretty girl who had a wee dog that jumped through hoops. It was doing really well until a lot of people down the front started making barking noises. Even from where we were standing, we could see that the poor wee soul had pissed and shat on the stage with fright before shooting off the stage followed by the pretty girl who was crying and calling the barkers a bunch of bastards. Everybody started laughing and laughed even more when a man came on doing cartwheels, put one of his hands right in the dog's piss and shit, slipped and landed on his arse. While he was being helped off, the man with the fancy waistcoat and bowler hat walked on and wiped up the mess before the other turns came on. Finally, the woman who had been singing when we came in came back on and started singing again. Everybody joined in again.

"Come on, Willie, time to go" said Goose. We walked through the door and down the stairs. The man wasn't there any more so we carried on down till we reached the street. It had started to get dark so Goose took my hand as we ran through the alley into

30

the Trongate and along to the alley at the top of Old Wynd.

We had only just got through the alley when I heard my mother shouting for me.

"I'm here, mammy" I shouted in reply and headed down towards my house.

"See you later, wee man," said Goose as he turned and went back through into the Trongate.

That was the first time I was ever in the Britannia Music Hall, but Goose and I went there a lot after that. Sometimes the man with the fancy waistcoat and the bowler hat would be standing at the door or the doors would be closed so we couldn't go in and we would just have to sit in the alley and listen to the songs. Goose knew a lot of them and he taught me the words so that we could sing along together, especially when we managed to skip in which we did most weeks.

Chapter Five

Conspiracy and Resolution

The following Saturday morning, Goose brought his mother round to our house. As usual, it was raining, not heavily, just drizzle, but I was still kept in because my mother always said that it was the 'wee rain' that got through your clothes and gave you a chill.

We were sitting by the fire when we heard someone knocking on the door. When my mother opened the door, I heard a voice say "Mrs McCart? I'm Annie Lavery, Isaac's mother." "Isaac?" I heard my mother say quizzically until she caught sight of Goose standing beside his mother. "Oh, come on in Mrs Lavery", she said as she ushered them into the room. When I looked at Goose's mother, I thought she looked nothing like him. While Goose had a fresh rosy face and blond curly hair, his mother's face was quite dark and she had long, straight black hair. She was wearing a long, shiny, green dress and the shawl around her shoulders was totally unlike the black, woollen shawls that nearly all of the local women wore. This shawl was mainly a shiny red but with other bright-coloured patterns and gold-coloured tassels hanging from the edges.

My mother asked her to sit down, motioning her to my father's chair and asked if she would like a cup of tea.

"That would be lovely," replied Mrs Lavery "And, if you don't mind, perhaps we could have this with it," she added as she reached into her bag and brought out a big clootie dumpling.

"My, that would be grand," my mother said as she took the dumpling and put it on the table.

When the tea had been made and some slices of dumpling, which was still quite hot, were handed out, the two women started chatting and Goose gave me a nod with just the beginnings of a grin. My mother thanked Mrs Lavery for the gifts that she had sent round and told her that she thought that her Isaac was a fine boy with good manners and that he was a credit to her and her husband.

"Aye, he is thank you very much. He's been telling me and his da that he really likes coming round here to play with your boy, Willie is it?" she replied. Then she added "Is it only the one you've got?"

I thought I saw a slight look of sadness in my mother's eyes as she nodded and said "Aye, just the one."

Mrs Lavery must have noticed the look in my mother's eyes because she told my mother that she had had five children but that two of them, a boy and a girl, had died just after they were born. My mother then told her about Lizzie and wee Mary Ann and they both spoke about how terrible it was that so many wee souls died without ever having had a chance to grow up.

The two women chatted away, talking about all sorts of boring stuff and in no time at all they were calling each other by their first names like they had known each other for ages.

Since I was becoming bored, I asked if Goose and I could go out and play. The rain forgotten and with a new pal to gossip with, my mother said that that would be alright, as did Mrs Lavery.

Armed with another two slices of dumpling, Goose and I escaped and headed up into the alley and out of the rain. There we sat, eating the dumpling and talking about what had happened in the Britannia the previous Sunday, especially about the wee dog. Needless to say, this sent us into fits of laughter; even more so when Goose tried to do a cartwheel and also landed on his arse.

I asked Goose who the man with the fancy waistcoat and the bowler hat was.

"I think his name is Mr Ferguson," he replied. "As far as I know he runs the place and is the chucker-out. One time, I was sitting in the alley listening to the singing because the doors were closed when suddenly they flew open and a man fell out into the street. Mr Ferguson was behind him and told him to get to fuck and not to come back. The man shouted back 'Fuck you, Ferguson and fuck your hoor of a wife as well'. That's how I know his name is Ferguson."

As I began to ask Goose what a 'hoor' was he held up his hand and carried on. "Well, the next thing is, Mr Ferguson goes inside and comes out with a big, flat, iron bar. You know the ones that they put on the doors with a padlock?" he asked.

When I nodded, he continued,

"Well he walks over to where the man is still lying in the street and wallops him right across the face with it. I think he broke his nose cause there was blood everywhere. 'Fuck me and fuck my wife' he shouted as he started to kick the man between the legs about four or five times, 'you'll no be fucking anybody for a long time to come. And if I ever see you round here again, I'll leave you with no balls at all, ya bastard.'"

Completely forgetting about asking Goose what a 'hoor' was, I asked him what happened to the man.

"Oh he was lying there moaning and holding his balls, but I didn't want to hang around too long so I picked up some pennies that had fallen out of his pockets and took off."

"Do you think Mr Ferguson will hit us with the iron bar if he catches us skipping in" I asked, worriedly.

"No. The most we'll get is a kick on the arse or a good skelp on the lug." he replied with a laugh. A smack on the ear or a kick on the arse I could handle. It wouldn't be the first time I'd had that, especially from my father. The conversation then returned to the different turns we had seen the week before.

After what seemed like a few minutes but was, in fact, a couple of hours, I heard my mother shouting for me so we went back to the house. When we got there, Goose's mother was at the top of the stairs saying cheerio to my mother and telling her to mind and come round to her house in the Saltmarket when she got the chance. My mother promised her that she would and started thanking her again for her gifts and for the clootie dumpling but Mrs Lavery insisted that it was no bother at all. She came downstairs, ruffled my hair and gave me a wink and a grin.

"See you soon, Willie."

Then, with Goose in tow, she headed up the Wynd to the Trongate.

When I got into the house, my mother already had the two big pots on the range and was peeling some spuds for our supper.

"Sure," she said "that Mrs Lavery is a fine woman and no mistake. Do you know that she only wants to take you with her when her and her man are going to the docks just so you can see all the big boats."

"And can I?"

"Of course, Willie. You know that I would like to take you myself, but a woman can't go down that way unless she's got her man with her and I don't think I could get your da to go."

I was delighted and immediately started dreaming about going around with Goose and his mother and seeing all the black men and Indians and chinks. Having already seen a black man, I wondered what an Indian and a chink looked like. In fact, I was really wondering what an Indian or a chink *was* and I reminded myself to ask Goose the next time I saw him. I didn't ask my mother because she would have asked me why I wanted to know and I was sure that Mrs Lavery hadn't said anything about that part of going down the docks.

When my father came home, my mother was all excited as she told him about her visitor but, interestingly, she didn't say anything about the docks. My father, who had never met Goose, gave a shrug and sat down on his chair, took off his boots and lit his pipe.

Later, as we were eating, my mother started talking about Mrs Lavery and Goose again.

"For fuck's sake, Mary Ann," he shouted banging his knife and fork down on the table, "I'm not fucking interested in Mrs fucking Lavery or her fucking duck. Now give me a fucking wink of peace to have my supper."

I could see that my mother was upset about what he had said but, thankfully, she didn't answer back. Although my mother could have a rough edge to her tongue when she wanted, she was also aware of the consequences of setting him off again. Consequences for her and also for me since I would, no doubt, have been included in any further outbursts of anger.

The rest of the meal was finished in silence and my mother cleared the plates and cups away. Since it was now the time for my father's bath, I went out and sat on the stairs. As I sat there, I could feel the tears trying to get out of my eyes, but I held them in. I felt sorry for my mother as she had had a very nice day up till then and now it had probably been totally wasted. I also knew that if he was in a bad mood now, he would be ten times worse when he came home from the pub that night. I was not looking forward to lying in bed with my mother, waiting for him to come staggering home. Hopefully, when he came home, he would think we were asleep although I also knew that, if he was in a bad enough temper, he would think nothing of waking us, and half the neighbours, with his shouting and bawling.

I remember thinking to myself that my father was a big bastard and that, when I grew up, I wouldn't let him shout at my mother or hit her ever again. I imagined myself as Mr Ferguson and using the big flat iron bar to batter my father to make him stop upsetting or hitting my mother. I also revisited the promises that I had made to myself that, when *I* was a man, *I* wouldn't ever treat *my* wife like that and that my *own* children would always be happy and wouldn't have to worry when I came home drunk because *I* wouldn't be like my father.

Chapter Six

Sisters and Mothers

I hated school. Every day I would tell my mother that I didn't want to go, but she insisted, because she said that she would get into trouble if I didn't. To get to the school we had to walk down to the bottom of the Wynd, along Bridgegate Street, down the Saltmarket and right along Greendyke Street past the Green till, we reached the school, which was beside a big timber yard. In the good weather, the walk was fairly pleasant, but, when it was raining, which seemed to be most of the time, we were usually soaked through by the time we got there. I was always feeling so miserable that I didn't even realise that my poor mother had to make this trek four times each day since she had to come and get me when the school finished.

All the teachers, including the headmistress, were nuns who lived in a convent in Charlotte Street, which was the street before the school. All the children were terrified by these mysterious figures dressed in strange black dresses with their faces framed in white. Apart from their size, the only way I could tell them apart was by focussing on particular features in their faces. My teacher, Sister Mary Veronica, had a front tooth missing, which meant that she let out a whistling sound whenever she said a word with an 's' in it. On one of my first days in class John Mulgrew, who lived near us in the Wynd, gave a whistle each time that she did and she went mad. She couldn't see who was doing it because there were so many of us in the class and John was in the middle somewhere. Because she had a rough idea of where the sound was coming from, she walked over and started hitting everybody on the head with a long wooden pointer. The children who were struck were crying while others were trying to get away from her. However, we were so tightly packed together that there was no escape and quite a few were left with a sore head. John wasn't one of them.

After a few minutes, things calmed down and she resumed the lesson. Almost immediately, she gave another whistle and John did the same thing again. Grabbing the pointer, she made to the general area again. However, before she could start hitting heads again, Michael Doyle, who had been hit the first time around, stood up and shouted "Please, sister, it was him" as he pointed at John. She grabbed John by his hair and dragged him to the front of the class.

"What's your name, boy?" she demanded.

Shaking like a leaf, he replied "John Mulgrew, sister."

"Well, John Mulgrew, hold your hands out like this" she said holding her arms straight out, one hand on top of the other with palms upwards. When John did this, she opened her desk, which looked a bit like the pulpit in the chapel, and took out a leather belt, which was split into three at one end. Standing in front of John, she lifted the belt and brought it down with an almighty crack on his hand. John let out a scream and tucked his hand under his armpit but she told him to hold them out again with the hand that had been underneath now on top and she hit him again. Despite his screams and accompanying tears, she repeated this process until she had hit him six times. When finished, she moved another boy from the front of the class to John's place and John had to sit at the front. He sobbed and cried for quite some time after that while the lessons went on.

The leather belt, which was called a tawse, was brought out several times on a daily basis. Any wrongdoing whatsoever, from being late to talking in class, was mercilessly punished and woe betide any child who drew his hands away as she swung the strap, as that would lead to a doubling-up of the punishment. I believe that the first "big" words I ever learned were "there will be sustained quietness and instantaneous obedience", which were written on a notice on the wall of the class.

If you wanted to ask anything you had to hold your hand up and wait for Sister Mary Veronica to see you. This included asking for permission to go to the toilet. Sometimes, a child would leave it too late to attract her attention and would piss himself or, worse, shit in his trousers. Far from being sympathetic, she would make the poor unfortunate stand in a corner wringing with piss or stinking of shit until the end of the class. At times, due to the general poor health amongst the children, there could be as many as five or six of them caught in these unfortunate circumstances. Thankfully, I never had to suffer this indignity, although I was not totally immune from classroom embarrassment.

My own inglorious moment came following a momentary lapse when I was caught whispering to the boy who shared a desk with me. Without warning, I felt a hand grasping my hair and I was pulled from my seat. Steeling myself for the coming punishment, I was astonished when she let go of my hair and let out a shriek.

"You dirty, filthy disgusting boy!" she shouted as she slapped furiously at her own hand. "Get out of my sight" she added pointing towards the door. I opened the door and stepped out into the narrow corridor and waited, wondering what it was that I might be guilty of.

When the headmistress, Mother Mary Francis, came down the corridor ringing the bell to signal the end of classes for the day, she drew me a withering look and demanded to know why I had been sent outside.

"Please, Mother Mary Francis, I don't know."

"Don't know, don't know" she repeated her voice rising with each 'don't know'. "I'll teach you don't know." Just when I thought she was going to give me a slap, or worse, clatter me with the bell, Sister Mary Veronica came out of the classroom and told her that she would have to speak to my mother as my hair was full of lice.

"Is that all," I thought. That was nothing unusual. As far as I knew everybody had lice in their hair and in their clothes as well, but I knew better than to say this. I knew better than to say anything at all, so I stood there with my head bowed.

I was told to stay where I was while Sister Mary Veronica went outside to fetch my mother, who would be waiting for me. When my mother came in she looked angrier than I had ever seen her before and, by the way she looked at me, she was thinking that I had done something really wrong. I followed my mother and Sister Mary Veronica to the headmistress's room. When we got there, Mother Mary Francis scolded my mother for letting me come to school with my hair in such a state. She reminded her that it was a privilege for a child to come to school. She added that, when she was a child, her parents appreciated that privilege and always made sure that she was clean, tidy, respectful and hard-working when they sent her to school.

I thought I could see my mother getting angry again and I could see the beginning of tears in her eyes. However, she did not answer back, as that would have been unthinkable. Instead, she stood, head bowed, apologising and promising that this would not happen again.

"See that it doesn't or this boy will not be allowed to return to this school and I will have to inform the church authorities of that fact." As she said this, she gave a dismissive wave and we went out, my mother gripping my hand so hard it hurt, but I didn't complain.

"Oh, Willie, what am I going to do? If I don't send you to school, me and your da will get into trouble. I can wash your hair but I can't get all the wee nits out because your hair is so curly."

I asked her what nits were and she told me that they were like wee eggs and that they turned into

43

lice so, even with my hair washed, there would be more lice there the next day.

She was so preoccupied that she forgot to cut across the Green to the fish market to get the fish for our supper and I had to remind her that it was Friday. Cutting across the Esplanade towards the market, she told me that the best thing would be to ask my father when he came home from work.

"Ask my da." I thought to myself, dreading his reaction when she told him what had happened. No doubt I would get the blame and be lucky to escape a clout.

Chapter Seven

Cut and Trust

As it turned out, my father seemed totally unconcerned and told my mother to take me round to her father who would be able to fix me. I wondered what my grandfather would be able to do but I had no doubt that, like my other grandfather, he could do anything.

"Right, James. I'll take him round after our supper," my mother replied, relieved that my father had, indeed, found the answer to their problem.

When we had finished our supper my father lit his pipe and settled back in his chair while my mother cleared away the plates and cups. She wet a cloth and wiped my face and hands, brushed her hair and put her shawl round her shoulders. By that time, my father had dozed off in his chair, as he almost always did, so she took the pipe out of his mouth and put it on the mantelpiece before we set off for my grandfather's house in the Back Wynd. We walked down to about halfway in our Wynd, then we made our way through closes and yards to New Wynd, before crossing and passing through another close and across a yard till we reached the back yard of the building where my grandfather lived.

Avoiding the shit pile in the middle, we crossed the yard. When we reached his door my mother gave a quick knock and we went in. My grandmother, Lizzie, was at the sink, washing dishes while my grandfather, James, was sitting in his chair puffing on his pipe. Their wee dog, which had been lying in front of the fire, ran over to me and started jumping up and down till I bent down to give him a pat. My grandfather was always telling me that Wolfe was the best rat catcher in the whole world. When I had asked him why he called such a wee dog Wolfe he told me it was named after a man and not after a real wolf.

My grandmother made a cup of tea and gave me a biscuit. When my mother told my grandfather what had happened, he started to curse and to say something about the nuns but my grandmother told him to "shush in front of the boy" and he did as he was told. After everyone had finished their tea, my grandfather told me to sit on one of his wooden chairs while he opened a cupboard and brought out his clippers, which he often used to cut my hair.

"I'm sorry about this, Willie son," he said as he started to cut. I was a little confused because he had never said "sorry" any other time that he had given me a haircut. Gradually, however, I realised that there seemed to be more hair than usual landing on the floor and, after a few minutes, there was a circle of red curls around the chair. When he had finished, I put my hand to my head and, realising that there was almost no hair there for me to feel, I burst into tears.

"There, there, Willie son," my grandmother said as she gathered me in her arms and held me to her tightly. "It'll soon grow back" she said soothingly.

"Aye it will but we'll have to keep it short while you're at the school" my grandfather said from his chair.

I know I was less than happy to hear this but I must have realised that my grandfather must have acted for the best and I walked over and climbed up on his knee. He gave me a big hug and I was surprised to see a single tear running down his cheek.

"But, granda, everybody will be calling me 'baldy'," I sobbed.

"Sticks and stones will break my bones but names will never hurt me," chanted my grandfather.

"That's all well and good, James, but he's only a wee boy and names *do* hurt wee boys," my grandmother argued. She then opened one of her cupboards and brought out an old flat cap belonging to my grandfather and she asked my mother to get her sewing box from below the bed. With the scissors she took from the box, she cut a section out from the back of the cap and then she started to sew the cut section together. It seemed to be no time at all till she was finished and she put the cap on my head. It was still a bit too big, but she said I would grow into it.

"At least your head will be kept warm," my mother said.

Although the cap was old, sweat-stained and not particularly clean, I didn't mind as it had the same familiar smell as my grandfather.

We stayed on for a short time. My mother and my grandmother were chatting about who had died, who was getting married and other such gossip while my grandfather was telling me stories. I asked him to tell me the one about Jack and the Beanstalk and, when he reached the part about the goose that laid the golden eggs, I told him about my new pal. I didn't tell him anything about what we had been doing though. He told me that he thought that this Goose fellow sounded like a good boy and my mother told him that he was right and that Goose's mother was a grand woman too.

When it came time for us to go home, my grandfather said he would walk some of the way with us. When he noticed that we were leaving, Wolfe became very excited and ran towards the door. My grandfather took a piece of rope and tied it round Wolfe's neck.

"Can't be too careful," he said. "If he smells a rat, he'll be off and I'm getting too old to chase after him."

After my grandmother gave me a big hug and a kiss, we walked out of the door and started on our way home. While we were walking across the yard, my grandfather asked my mother about my First Communion. She told him that I would be making it in three weeks, on the first Sunday in May.

"You know, Willie, when your ma made her First Communion about eight years after we came to Glasgow from Fermanagh, your granny made her communion dress herself out of her own wedding dress because we couldn't afford to buy a new one. But I'll tell you one thing, she was the prettiest girl out of the whole lot." "Oh, da, you're embarrassing me," said my mother and she giggled like a little girl. When I looked at her, I saw that she had gone a little red in the face and, just for a moment, I imagined her, not as my mother, but as my grandfather's wee girl all dressed in white, hands joined in prayer and walking down to the altar rail to make her First Communion.

This thought was sharply interrupted by a loud yelp from Wolfe as he spotted a large rat scuttling across the close entrance at the other side of the yard. He almost pulled my grandfather off his feet as he made to chase the rat but, with an extreme effort, he managed to keep his feet and hold Wolfe back. However, Wolfe's yelp seemed to set all the other dogs in the area into a chorus of yelping and barking, accompanied by shouts and profanities from the inhabitants of the houses around the yard.

"Hey, Toner, for fuck's sake can you not get that fucking dog of yours to shut up. I've got to get up for my fucking work in the morning," a voice shouted from behind us. Turning round, my grandfather looked up at an open window and, recognising the owner of the voice, shouted back: "Sorry, Dessie. I'll try my best but you know what he's like when he spots a rat. I'll buy you a drink tomorrow night in Waxy's if you're in."

Seemingly placated, Dessie pulled his head back inside and pulled the window down.

When we got through the close into New Wynd, my grandfather said that he would take the long way round to avoid any chance of annoying anybody else. My mother said that we would walk with him up to the top and we could go our separate ways when we reached the Trongate. When we reached the top, I heard the music and singing from the Britannia. My grandfather started to whistle the tune that we could hear and I found myself wishing that it was Sunday night so that Goose and I could try and skip in again.

As we said goodnight and cheerio to my grandfather, he pulled the peak of my new old cap down over my eyes and turned to walk along to the alley at the top of Back Wynd. He had to pull Wolfe along as the dog was trying to follow us.

"Good night, granda. Good night, Wolfe," I shouted.

"Good night, Willie, and Wolfe says 'good night' too" my grandfather shouted back.

When we got home, my father was already in bed, fast asleep. As quietly as possible, we got ready for bed and climbed in. In spite of my silent objections, my mother managed to get my cap off my head and dropped it off the side of the bed. I made a mental note to myself to check it tomorrow just as I had to check my shoes each morning to ensure that a cockroach or some other insect hadn't crawled inside during the night, as often happened.

Chapter Eight

Carriages and Kings

The next morning we all got up at six o'clock as usual. While my father was getting ready for work, my mother was cleaning out the ashes from the bottom of the fire, which was still lit from the day before and waiting for the kettle to boil. I carried the bucket with the hot ashes outside and left it on the landing to cool. Later, it would be taken and emptied onto the shit pile in the yard.

My father had some bread and cheese and a cup of tea and left for his work at half past six. After he left, my mother and I had our breakfast and then I helped her to tidy up. Because it was Saturday and my father had got his wages the day before, my mother got me ready and we walked down to the market, after I insisted on turning back for my cap, to buy some food for the week, mostly potatoes and some other vegetables. If my mother was making meat for us, then she would usually buy it on the day she was using it in case it went off.

When we got back home, I was surprised and delighted to see Goose and his mother standing on the landing at our door. Mrs Lavery and my mother said hello to each other and Mrs Lavery asked my mother if it would be alright for me to go with her down to the docks that day. My mother said that that would be fine, but that I would have to be back home before my father returned from work. Mrs Lavery told her that she would have me back by four o'clock. We said cheerio to my mother and started walking down the Wynd towards Bridgegate.

"Where did you get the bunnet, wee man," asked Goose, tapping the peak with his finger.

"My granny made it for me," I replied and proceeded to tell him about what had happened at school and about my unwanted haircut.

"Ach, that's a shame," said Mrs Lavery. "I've got some stuff that I use on my wee ones which kills all the nits. I'll send some round to your ma and that way you'll be able to keep your curls when they grow back in", she added.

I was delighted and thanked her, but I wished that my mother had had this stuff the day before.

When we reached Bridgegate, Goose pointed to a man sitting on a four-wheeled cart and said "There's my da."

The cart was the strangest one I had ever seen. It had yellow wheels and all the wood was decorated with paintings of flowers in lots of bright colours, including green, yellow, red and blue. In addition, there was a strange, metal, triangular frame attached from one end to the other on the top of the cart. Unusually, even the harness fixing the horse, which was light brown, to the cart, was decorated with brass badges and coloured tassels. The load on the cart was made up of bags and boxes. A dark-haired girl, who looked about my age was sitting on one of the boxes behind Goose's father.

"Willie, this is Mr Lavery," said Goose's mother.

"Hello there, Willie, climb on up" said Mr Lavery as he leant over, his hand outstretched. I put my left foot on a wheel and took his hand and was whisked up on to the bed of the cart, where I was soon joined by Goose and his mother.

"This is my wee sister Annie," said Goose. "And this is my wee brother, Peter," he added pointing to a small wooden box right behind his father. When I looked into the box, I saw a baby who was fast asleep.

"You and Isaac sit beside Ben," said Mrs Lavery as she sat down next to Annie and Peter. After Goose and I had sat down, Mr Lavery, giving the reins a shake, shouted "Off we go, Sandy" and the horse set off at a slow and gentle pace.

Although the first part of the journey was familiar, since it was along the same route that led to the chapel, it looked completely new when viewed from the moving cart. I had been on many carts, before but only as places to play and never when hitched to a horse. However, before we could get out of Bridgegate, we had to wait until a herd of cattle was driven past on the way to the slaughterhouse.

"Looks like the Belfast boat is in early, Annie," said Mr Lavery "More work for our Peter."

Goose explained to me that his father's brother, Peter, was a skinner who worked in the slaughterhouse. He also told me that his grandfather and all the Lavery men were skinners, although his own father only did that work for a couple of months of the year.

Finally, the cattle herd passed and Mr Lavery guided the cart into Clyde Street and we rumbled along on the cobbles in amongst all the other carts and carriages going along the street in both directions, while others were also going in both directions to and from Stockwell Street and the bridge across the river. Because it had not been raining for a couple of days, the air was full of dust and I noticed Goose's mother covering the baby's box with a muslin cloth. She handed me another cloth and told me to cover my nose and mouth. I noticed that Mr Lavery and Goose had already done this with cloths that they had had around their necks.

"So, Willie, you want to go and see all the big boats," said Mr Lavery, raising his voice to be heard above the street noises.

"Oh aye," I replied not even attempting to disguise my excitement as I looked up at him. He looked bigger than my father and his hands holding the reins seemed to be massive. I had heard people talking about someone having 'hands like shovels' and this seemed to perfectly describe Mr Lavery's hands. From what I could see outside of his cap, his hair looked like Goose's, blonde and curly. Even from the side, I could see that his nose seemed to be an odd shape and he had lots of little scars on his face.

"You know, Willie, my ancestors came to Ireland in big boats hundreds of years ago. They were called Vikings and my family were the kings. I'll let you into a little secret," he continued, his voice dropping to a conspiratorial whisper. "I am really King Benedict and Goose is Prince Isaac, but you can't tell anyone just now until it's time for us to go back.

When that happens, you can come and live in our royal palace."

The thought of living in a palace such as I had heard described in many of the stories told by my grandfather was my idea of a dream come true.

"When will that be and can my ma and da come as well?" I asked, excitedly.

"Oh that will be a long time yet. We have to wait until the English have left first but, when they do, your ma and da, your grandas and grannies, your uncles and aunties and all your cousins will all be welcome to come with you."

Although I was delighted to hear this, I was a little confused. I had heard of the English but had never heard of the Vikings. When I told him this, he explained that the Vikings came from countries called Norway and Denmark and that they were fierce warriors who had conquered parts of Scotland, England and Ireland. When he added that they didn't bother to conquer Wales because there was nothing worth taking there, Mrs Lavery punched him lightly on the back.

"Ben Lavery, you didn't think that when you were begging me to marry you," she laughed.

"What are you talking about? I said there was nothing worth having *then* but when there *was*, this particular Viking came and took it," he replied answering her laugh with one of his own. "Besides, you haven't lived in Wales since you were ten years old."

Goose gave me a nudge and tapped his index finger to the side of his head as if to say that his mother and father were daft although he, too, had a broad grin on his face.

As we were passing the chapel I told Goose that I would soon be making my First Holy Communion there on the first Sunday in May. On hearing this, Mrs Lavery said that that would be a great day for me and my family.

"We'll have to try and get to see that, Ben," she said to her husband.

"We certainly will," he replied. "If you find out the time of the Mass and tell Goose, then we'll all try to come and see you," he added, putting his hand on my shoulder.

I wasn't sure if I believed them or not, since Goose had told me that they didn't go to chapel any more, but I kept my doubts to myself.

Once we had passed the chapel, I began to see the tops of some big boats behind the sheds on our left hand side. I could also see two pubs to our right. I asked Goose's father if he was going into those pubs. Mr Lavery shook his head and, pointing to a large grey building with four pillars and two flagpoles, one sticking out in front and one at the top, he said "We don't do any business around here, Willie, because that building is full of robbers working for the government. Every chance they get, they steal from hard-working, honest men like myself and give the money to their bosses."

When I asked who their bosses were he replied "Sure that's only the Customs House over there and their bosses are all sitting down there at the parliament in London with the biggest boss of the lot, Queen Victoria."

To my young mind, it seemed to be most unfair that somebody like Queen Victoria, whom I thought to be the richest person in the whole world, should be stealing money off Mr Lavery. When I said this to Mr Lavery, he gave a broad grin and said "And how do you think she got to be the richest person in the world, Willie? I'll tell you how. It's because her and all the kings and queens before her have been robbing ordinary people for hundreds of years, not only in Glasgow but all over the world..."

Before he could go any further Goose's mother broke in "That's enough, Ben, Willie's a wee bit young for that stuff."

"Maybe so but he'll learn soon enough that the world is made up of us poor souls at the bottom and that bunch of bas... bandits at the top."

Chapter Nine

The Spirit of Ireland

After a few minutes, we reached the end of Clyde Street, at the junction with Jamaica Street and Glasgow Bridge. There were so many carts, carriages, Menzies Tartan omnibuses and people going in so many directions that it took us over five minutes to get across to the Broomielaw. While crossing I could see that the other side of the river across the bridge was lined with what seemed to be a never-ending line of ships. I could also see lots of cranes swinging their loads to the docks at the other side of the ships.

When we had crossed, Mr Lavery turned the cart to the right into a small lane and then stopped. Wee Peter had started crying and Mrs Lavery picked him up.

"I think the wee one's hungry, Ben," she said and she opened her shawl to hold the baby to her chest.

"I'll take the boys with me," Mr Lavery said, jumping down from the cart. Goose and I jumped down to join him. He walked to the back of the cart and lifted a large leather bag which was hanging on the back. Reaching under the cart, he brought out a sack from a sort of iron cage fixed to the bottom. I noticed that there was a large bundle of white cloth and some leather cases in the cage as well. He opened the sack and pulled out several handfuls of hay which he put into the leather bag.

"That's Sandy's dinner," said Goose as his father hung the bag over the horse's head so that his mouth was inside.

"Right, boys, off we go," said Mr Lavery as he took our hands and led us through the traffic to the other side of the street and into a large building. Inside, there seemed to be hundreds of people sitting, standing or moving around. Pushing through the crowd, Mr Lavery led us to an opening at the other side and it was there that I got my first close-up view of a steamboat. It didn't look as high as some of the other ships that I could see on both sides of the river, but it was still a lot bigger than any of the other boats that I had seen further up the river. It was painted black except for a broad red stripe near the top and there were a lot of rust patches all over the side that I could see. There was one large funnel which was putting out a lot of black smoke. The wind was blowing the smoke all over the place and I could feel it stinging my eyes. There were two wooden ramps leading from the boat to the dockside and a few people were coming down off the boat.

"Wait here, boys," said Mr Lavery as he walked off towards the back of the boat.

"Where's your da going?" I asked Goose.

"Oh my da's got a couple of pals who work on that boat and they bring him stuff over from Belfast."

"What do they bring him," I asked.

"I'm not supposed to tell anyone, but if you cross your heart and hope to die if you tell anybody else, then I'll tell you."

Eager to find out what the big secret was I duly crossed my heart and swore to keep the secret.

"It's stuff called poteen. A lot of Irish people over here love the stuff, but you can only get it in Ireland," he informed me, almost in a whisper.

"But what is it?" I whispered back.

"I think it's something like whisky, but they don't sell it in the pubs. My da usually passes it on to Waxy Mulligan who sells it in his shebeen."

Before I could question him further, his father came back carrying a wooden box which looked quite heavy. He motioned for us to follow him and we set off through the crowd. When we reached the street outside, I saw that a lot of people were walking up and down outside the building carrying bundles and bags and looking lost. Quite a few of them were talking in a language that I didn't understand. When I asked Goose what it was, he told me that they were just off the boat and were speaking Irish and that some of them probably couldn't speak any English at all. Staying close to Mr Lavery, we crossed over the street to the lane and back to the cart. Mr Lavery put the box on the cart and climbed up. He opened the box and took out four stone jars which he laid down on their sides inside the baby's box before covering them with a blanket.

It looked like Wee Peter must have finished eating because he was now being held by his sister, Annie.

Goose's mother was filling two baskets with plants and small dolls made of straw. Getting down from the cart, she put her shawl on top of her head so that it hung down over her shoulders and lifted the two baskets. By this time, Mr Lavery had got back down from the cart and also had two baskets which he hung either end of a wooden yoke which was across his shoulders. I couldn't see what was in his baskets, as they had covers over them.

"Goose, you stay with Willie just now and keep an eye on the cart and on your brother and sister. If anybody gets hungry, there's some bread and cheese and milk in the usual place. We'll be back in a couple of hours to feed the baby."

Waving cheerio, Mr and Mrs Lavery walked back down the lane and turned to their right into the Broomielaw.

I was bursting with questions for Goose about everything I had seen. When I asked him about the stuff under the cart and about his mother and father's baskets, his wee sister said that I was awful nosey. Goose told her to be quiet, but he was smiling as he spoke to her. He explained that the white cloth was a tent that his father put over the metal frame on the back of the cart when it was raining so that everybody and all the stuff on the cart would be kept dry.

"Sometimes, if we're working outside Glasgow and we can't get anywhere to stay, we sleep in it as well. The bags underneath have got pots and plates and spoons and stuff so that we can have something to eat" he added.

"That sounds like good fun," I replied thinking that that would be like having an adventure.

"Usually it's not bad but sometimes it can be a wee bit uncomfortable if we've collected a lot of stuff because that means that there's not much room for us."

"And his feet are usually stinking as well" Annie said ducking as Goose pretended to slap her. Her sudden movement disturbed wee Peter and he started to cry. Annie rocked him in her arms and hummed a wee tune to calm him.

When he had settled down again, she put him in his box and covered him with another blanket. Goose then told me about the plants and the dolls in his mother's basket. He explained that the plants were heather and that his mother sold them and the dolls to the foreign sailors who drank in the pubs, because they believed that they would bring them good luck. His father's baskets had a lot of different stuff in them, mostly cheap jewellery and trinkets.

"He sometimes sells tobacco, but that's a secret as well," he added. Again, I promised to keep my mouth shut.

"I'm starving. Anybody else hungry?" Goose asked.

When Annie and I both answered that we were, Goose opened a small sliding door underneath the seat and brought out the bread and cheese along with a small metal can which had milk in it.

"Help yourselves," he said, putting everything in front of us. For a few moments we ate in silence then passed the can around so that we all got a drink.

"Could you be sparing a little of that for some poor travellers," a voice said from the back of the cart. Surprised, the three of us looked towards the direction of the voice. I saw a man holding a large bundle tied with string and a woman carrying a baby. I looked at Goose to see what he would say. He lifted two pieces of bread and a small piece of cheese and went down to the end of the cart.

"That's all we can spare. We've got to keep some for my ma and da," he said handing them to the man.

"God bless you, son," the woman said. "We've just got off the boat and we've not had anything to eat since we left Belfast." The man gave the woman a piece of bread and broke the cheese and gave her half. Goose told them that they could get some water from a well round the side of the steamboat building across the road. They thanked him again and turned to go. Before they left, they asked Goose if he could tell them where Portugal Street was. Goose said that he had never heard of it. However, when the man mentioned that he had been told it was in a place called Gorbals, Goose said that all they had to do was cross over the bridge and they would be in the Gorbals and that somebody would be able to tell them where Portugal Street was.

"Thanks again, son," the man said as they set off.

"No problem, mister. As my da says 'we Irish have got to help each other as no other bugger will'" said Goose as he waved goodbye to the man and his family.

Chapter Ten

Pick a Bale of Cotton

When Goose's mother and father came back, their baskets were empty. Mrs Lavery fed wee Peter while Mr Lavery had some bread and cheese. Goose, Annie and I also had a bit more to eat as well. When everyone had finished, Mrs Lavery took Annie across to the steamer building to get water. When they came back Mr Lavery gave me and Goose two empty sacks each, jumped down off the cart and told us to follow him. The three of us walked round the corner into the Broomielaw. We walked some distance along until we reached Anderston Quay. As we passed all the pubs on our right hand side, I could hear lots of noise, mostly singing but also the sounds of arguments. We had just passed one pub, the King's Arms, when we heard a commotion behind us. A group of men had tumbled out of the pub and were shouting and throwing punches at each other. Most people just walked on past the fight and all the carts and traps on the street continued on their way. Some of the drivers shouted words of encouragement to the combatants as well as a lot of good-humoured insults. I asked Mr Lavery if they would get lifted by the Peelers but he said that the fight would soon be over and they would all go back into the pub. If anyone was left outside drunk or unable to get back into the pub, then he would probably be lifted if a Peeler should happen to pass by. He added that he thought this to be highly unlikely as the Peelers tended not to come down this way during the day.

About halfway along Anderston Quay, we crossed over to the dockside. There seemed to be hundreds of carts being loaded with bales of what I was told was cotton from America. There seemed to be a similar number of loaded carts going off in all directions.

"Where are they all going?" I asked Mr Lavery.

"Most of those ones will be going to the mills down Bridgeton way" he replied pointing to the carts heading in the direction we had come from. "Most of the others will be heading up to Port Dundas. The cotton will be put on the canal boats and be taken down to the mills in Lanarkshire."

"What's a canal?" I asked.

"They're just like rivers but they were dug out by hundreds of men and filled with water so that it would be easier to carry a lot of stuff from one part of the country to another."

"My auntie Peggy lives on a canal boat doesn't she, da" Goose said.

"Aye, that's right. Her and your uncle Duncan are on the Forth and Clyde. You wouldn't believe it, Willie, but our Peggy, Duncan and Goose's five cousins live in a tiny wee cabin on the boat. I don't know how they manage."

I couldn't imagine that the cabin would be any smaller than the house where I lived and I knew that some of the houses in the Wynds had just as many people living in them. When I said this, Goose started laughing.

"Listen, Willie, their cabin isn't even half the size of your house and all my cousins are older than me, but they all manage to squeeze in."

As we passed down the line of cotton ships, I noticed that most of the men carrying the bales down the gangways to the dockside, were black.

"I thought black men came from Africa" I said to Goose, confused since I had been told that these ships were from America. It was Mr Lavery who answered.

"Those men *are* from America, but their grandfathers were from Africa. They were captured and taken to America as slaves. All those men were once slaves as well, but they're free now since the war in America. A lot of them work on the cotton and tobacco ships, which used to belong to the Confederates, but have been taken over by the United States to help pay for the war."

It would be years later before I learned about the complicated history of what lay behind Mr Lavery's simple information but for then, I was satisfied with his explanation.

About the third or fourth ship down, Mr Lavery led Goose and me between two stacks of bales sitting on the quayside and we stood there for about five minutes until a man in a blue uniform with brass buttons came walking down the gangway. Mr Lavery took the sacks from Goose and me, told us to wait, and walked over to meet him. They shook hands and walked between two other stacks further down. While we were waiting, Goose told me about the time when his father had got into a fight with one of the men on a ship.

"A black man, who had been working on one of the cotton ships, had fallen off the gangway and into the water and my da helped him to get out. A man on another ship, I think it was from Cuba, but the man was American, shouted that he should have let the nigger drown since he and all his sambo brothers had taken the jobs of god-fearing, white men. My da told him to fuck off and mind his own business. The man came running down off the ship, but when he reached my da he didn't know what hit him. One punch and he went out like a light. What he didn't know is that my da is a boxer and spends a lot of the summer going round the fairs and earns money by fighting maybe nineteen or twenty people a day, so that man had no chance."

I couldn't imagine somebody fighting so many people. I had been involved in the usual childish scrapes, but they would only have involved two or three children at most.

"It must be great to be a good fighter," I said

"I'm a good fighter too" said Goose puffing out his chest. "My da taught me how to box. Even if you're fighting somebody bigger than you, you can beat them if you know how to box."

"Do you think he would teach me?" I asked.

"If you come round to my house and my da's in I'll ask him. I can show you some of the stuff as well but he's the best at it."

I liked the idea that I could beat someone who was bigger than me. I had come off second best in the past to bigger boys and, on one shameful occasion, to a bigger girl. I wasn't afraid to fight bigger boys; I just wasn't very good at it. Maybe Mr Lavery *would* be able to help.

After some time the two men came back carrying two sacks each. The man gave Goose and me one each and Mr Lavery kept hold of his two sacks. After they shook hands again and said a few words of goodbye, we headed off the quayside back to the street. The sacks that Goose and I were carrying were about half-full, but not very heavy. Mr Lavery's sacks, however, were nearly full, but he didn't seem to have any difficulty in carrying them.

"Right, boys, that's the work done for today and another good day's work it has been too. Well, Goose, do you think wee Willie's desperate to know what's in the sacks?"

"Well he's always asking questions about everything else so I wouldn't be at all surprised" he replied with a grin.

"No I don't" but secretly I was bursting with curiosity.

"Now it's a secret, Willie, so you can't tell anyone. When that ship comes to Glasgow the captain always brings me some tobacco, which he puts inside some of the cotton bales. I have to come down here to get it otherwise those robbers in the Customs House will be wanting to steal all my money off me."

"Cross my heart, Mr Lavery, I won't say a word, not even to my ma" I said earnestly, not wanting Queen Victoria to get his money.

"Good lad" he answered with a wink and a grin.

When we got back to the cart, we climbed up. Mr Lavery put the sacks in the boxes on the cart and got up on his seat. Once again, Goose and I sat beside him as we set off back home. When we arrived back at the bottom of Old Wynd, Mr Lavery stopped the cart. As I moved to get down to join Mrs Lavery and Goose who were already off the cart, Mr Lavery took a shiny silver three penny piece from a pouch and gave it to me.

"That's your wages for the day, son, and you'll get the same every time you come out to give us a hand." I stuttered a 'thank you' as, not counting the money Goose had given me, I had only ever been given such a sum two or three times before and then only on my birthday. I was also delighted by the knowledge that I was going to be able to go with them again

I waved goodbye to Mr Lavery and Annie who was holding wee Peter and set off with Goose and his mother up the Wynd towards my house. When we got there, my mother was standing by the railing. She waved to me and asked if I had a good time.

"It was great, mammy, and I can go again if I want," I answered excitedly.

"Aye but only if your ma says it's all right," Mrs Lavery insisted.

Seeing the pleading look on my face, my mother smiled and said that if I came back as happy as I seemed to be now, then I could go as often as I was asked. After a short chat with Mrs Lavery, my mother said that she would have to go in and start my father's dinner. After everyone had said their goodbyes, Mrs Lavery and Goose started walking back down the Wynd.

"See you tomorrow, Goose?" I shouted.

"No bother, wee man."

Before heading into the house I added my shiny three penny piece to the coppers in the hole in the wall, as I didn't think it would be a good idea to tell my mother what we had been doing.

That was just the first of many Saturday trips that I made with the Laverys and Mr Lavery, true to his word, gave me three pence every time I went. As time went on, Goose and I would even go into the pubs with his father or mother and help them to sell stuff. However, no matter how many times I went, I never ceased to be amazed by the sheer variety of people from so many different countries who were to be found round about the docks. Mr Lavery never seemed to tire in answering what must have seemed like incessant questioning from me about all the different countries that the people came from. I believe it would be true to say that, thanks to his information, I probably knew more about the geography and history of other countries than most other children of my age.

A big surprise for me, however, was that the whole Lavery family did indeed come to the chapel for my First Communion. I didn't see them until I was leaving the chapel in the procession with the other children and I got a sharp dig from Sister Mary

Veronica when I un-joined my hands to give them a slight wave. When I got home after the communion breakfast, my mother gave me a small medal with the Virgin Mary on it and told me that Goose's mother had asked her to give to me when she met her outside after the Mass.

Chapter Eleven

Dolley's Fixtures

One Wednesday, just before the school closed for the summer, my mother took me up to my other grandfather's in Bridgegate because it was his birthday. When we got there, my auntie Hannah answered the door. My auntie Hannah was really my father's auntie but, although she was married to my grandfather, she wasn't my grandmother. My real grandmother, Margaret, had died when my father was nine and my uncle Willie was four. My auntie Hannah who was my grandmother Margaret's sister had been working as a domestic servant in a big house somewhere in the south of Glasgow. I heard, when I was older, that she had had a baby girl, although she wasn't married and that she had gone to live in the Govan Poorhouse, which was in Eglinton Street and that the wee girl had died. When my grandmother Margaret died, my grandfather had gone to the Poorhouse and asked my auntie Hannah to come and look after my father and my uncle Willie, so that he could go to work. It seems that a priest had come to the house and told my grandfather that it wasn't right for my auntie Hannah to be living there like that and he insisted that either she moved out, or that she and my grandfather should get married, which is what they did.

Although my uncle Willie seemed to like my auntie Hannah, my father hated her and never stopped telling us this, especially when he had been drinking. I was on my father's side. Although I didn't hate her, I didn't like her at all. While my grandmother, Lizzie was always giving me cuddles and seemed to have a permanent smile on her face, my auntie Hannah's face always seemed to be tripping her, especially if my grandfather wasn't in. I had to sit up straight on a chair and I wasn't allowed to say anything unless I was spoken to. She seemed to spend most of her time sitting in a rocking chair puffing on a long, clay pipe. If my grandfather wasn't in, she used to criticise my mother a lot. She would say that my mother wasn't dressing me or bringing me up properly and that my father was a useless drunkard. I thought that my mother was scared of her because she never answered her back. It never occurred to me that the reason she kept her mouth shut was because my father would have gone mad if he found out and, given that he hated my auntie Hannah so much, would probably have gone straight down to their house and given her a right leathering and ended up in serious trouble with the Peelers.

When I spoke to my cousin, Helen, who was Uncle Willie's daughter, she told me that it was the same when she went there with my auntie Sarah Jane. Maybe it was because my auntie Hannah had lost her wee girl that she didn't like other children, but that was no excuse for the way she treated my mother and my auntie Sarah Jane.

Luckily, on that particular day, my grandfather was just in from his job at the waterworks. My mother had bought him some tobacco for his birthday and handed it to me to give to him.

"Happy birthday, granda," I said stretching out my arm and giving him the tobacco.

"Sure, isn't that a fine present that my favourite grandson is after giving me, Hannah?" he said, putting the tobacco on the table and lifting me off the floor in a tight hug.

"Hmm" was the reply accompanied by more of a grimace than a smile "But, Willie, you don't have any other grandsons," she added.

My grandfather gave her a withering look and told her to make herself useful and put the kettle on. While my mother was helping my auntie Hannah to make some tea, I was telling my grandfather about how I had been along to see all the big ships with my pal. I told him about all the different countries that the ships had come from and all the different people, ranging from the Irish to the black men working on the cotton ships from America that I had seen.

When I mentioned America, my grandfather said "You won't believe this Willie, but my da, your great granda, was in America once."

I was amazed. I knew that my mother and father had been born in Ireland and that it was quite far away, but to think that my great grandfather had been in America was something almost unbelievable.

Seeing the look of astonishment on my face, he continued, "Aye, your great grandfather, Mathew McCart, was a sergeant in the British Army during the war with the Americans which started about eight years before I was born."

"I didn't know that," my mother said. "James has never mentioned anything about it."

"That's because he's ashamed of it. He thinks that any Irishman who joins the British Army is a traitor. What he seems to forget is that the army was sometimes the only way that many young Irishmen could earn a living in those days. In fact it was the only way that a lot of young Scots, Welsh and English could earn a living as well. What he also forgets, but I don't, is that the majority of the landlords who allowed so many Irish people to die during the famine and who evicted them from their homes were, themselves, Irish. If the day ever comes when the Irish do the same as the Americans and kick the English out, I hope people remember that fact and do something about those bastards who are the real traitors."

This wasn't the first time that I had heard my grandfather talking about the landlords in Ireland. Every time he got on to the subject he would always seem to get really angry. At that time I was too young to understand but, since *he* said they were bastards and traitors, then that *had* to be the truth.

"Anyway, Willie, when my da was in America he met the wife of the President of the United States."

"What's a president?"

"The same as a king but different. You're a wee bit young to understand how they work over there so I'll not go into that just now. As I was saying, he met

Mrs Madison when he went to burn her house down."

When she heard this, my mother burst out laughing.

"Aye, it is funny, isn't it," my grandfather said with a broad grin, "but it's true, all the same. The army had reached Washington, which was the new capital city of the United States and my da was ordered to take a detachment of troops and burn down the White House, which was the home of the President and his family. As my da was leading his troops towards the house, he saw a lot of darkies carrying stuff out and putting it on a cart. He could see other carts away in the distance. Thinking, that there might be some valuable stuff left, he and his men hurried up to the house, but all that was there was furniture which was no good to them. They went into the house and had a good look about but there was only the odd bit of cutlery and other bits and pieces of no value. 'Excuse me, sergeant, said a grandly dressed woman who had come down a fancy staircase. Would you be so kind as to ask your men to help me carry something to my cart?' My da was astonished and speechless for a moment. I remember him telling me about how he couldn't believe her cheek. Even his men were grinning at him. 'And who might you be then?' he asked her.

'I am Dolley Payne Madison, the wife of the President of the United States of America' she replied proudly.

'And is your husband here, or has he run away like everybody else?'

'He is not here at the moment, but I can assure you, sergeant, that it will not be long before you and your comrades will be the ones running away. We've licked you before and we'll do it again, mark my words. In the meantime, will you be of assistance or not?'

My da, to his own surprise, detailed two men to help her carry out a giant portrait to the cart. When he asked Mrs Madison who the man in the portrait was, she told him that it was President George Washington, the general who had defeated the British in the Revolutionary War. My da burst out laughing and asked her not to tell that to his men otherwise he might get hanged for treason. When the portrait was safely tied to the cart, my da told Mrs Madison that she would have to leave as he had been ordered to burn the house down although he wasn't looking forward to doing it now, since it belonged to such a fine, brave woman.

'Makes no never mind, sergeant. When the war's over we'll build it bigger and better than it is now. However, that portrait is irreplaceable and I thank you kindly for your help. Before you burn the house, have a look in the cellar where you'll find something to help quench the thirst of you and your men. And take this for yourself' she said as she handed him a small silver snuff box and a silver dollar, which is the money that the Americans use. Once the Americans had left, the soldiers set fire to the house, but only after they had carried out quite a few bottles from the cellar, some of which they opened and drank from as they watched the flames take hold."

"My, that's some story" my mother said with a laugh. "That's even better than the ones that my da tells Willie about giants and fairies."

"But it's true" protested my grandfather. "And I'll prove it."

He reached under the bed and pulled out a small wooden box. Taking a key from his pocket, he used it to open the box and he took out a small cloth bag. He put his hand in the bag and when he drew it back out he was holding a small shiny box which had some fancy decoration on it.

"There you go. Look at that," he said turning the box upside down. Engraved on the bottom of the box was 'Dolley P.Madison' and, when he opened the box, there, inside, was a silver coin. He took the coin out and showed it to us. On one side was the word 'Liberty' and a woman's head with long hair and a number '1794' at the bottom. On the other side was a bird that my grandfather told me was an eagle. There was some writing round the edge of the coin but I couldn't read what it was.

"My da gave me these and I was going to give them to our James but since he is so ashamed of his granda then he's not getting them. Instead, when you're older, Willie, I'll give them to you and you'll be able to tell your children and grandchildren all about them. The only thing is that there might not be a United States of America by that time if they start fighting with each other again."

"What happened to my great granda?" I asked being too young to understand how valuable a gift I would be receiving and being more interested in finding out more about someone that nobody had mentioned before.

"He stayed in the army, but was shot in the shoulder during a battle with the Americans. Mrs Madison was right about the Americans winning again and the British Army went back up to Canada. Because of the damage to his shoulder, my da couldn't stay with the normal army and he was sent back to Ireland to join the veterans' battalion, which was on garrison duty in Enniskillen. It was there that he met and married my ma, your great granny. She died when I was only seven and her sister and her husband, my auntie Rose and my uncle Michael, looked after me when my da was on duty. By the time I married your granny, Margaret, in 1844, my da was a Chelsea pensioner in Kilmainham Hospital. His shoulder had got so bad over the years that they had to cut off his left arm and, because of that and his age, they sent him there. I never saw him again because we had to leave Ireland because of the famine the following year. I think he's probably dead by now."

As he said this his voice seemed to trail away and he had a faraway look in his eyes.

"Is that tea not ready yet?" he said to no-one in particular.

The tea was, indeed, ready and everyone had some. After putting everything back in the box and locking it, my grandfather made a great play of filling his pipe with the tobacco my mother had bought and puffing out great clouds of smoke after it was lit.

When we had finished our tea, my mother said that she would need to get home to make my father's dinner for him getting back from work. My grandfather gave both of us a big hug and thanked us again for his present. My auntie Hannah, as usual, gave a forced smile and said 'cheerio'. With that, we left and made our way along to the Wynd and up to our house. All my mother could talk about was the beautiful snuff box, while all I could think about was a lonely old man with an arm missing.

Chapter Twelve

Fighting Talk

For most of the rest of that year everything continued as before except for late June, all of July and August and the first two weeks in September, when all the Laverys left Glasgow to make their way around Scotland collecting and selling at the various fairs. I would have loved to go with them, but I knew that it would be a waste of time to ask my mother. Those months seemed to drag on forever without my pal and the visits to the docks.

However, there was still a lot of fun to be had for me and all the other Wynds children. This was particularly true during the demolition of the Slaughterhouse behind Jail Square. As soon as the work began, hundreds of rats poured out and scattered along Bridgegate and into the Wynds. At the bottom of the Wynds the squatters were killing them as fast as they could but quite a few made their way further up towards our house. All the children, and some of their mothers, armed with pieces of wood, heavy pans and various other weapons were trying to kill as many rats as possible to stop them getting into the numerous holes and gaps in the buildings. I even saw a woman with a spear and she was stabbing as many of the rats as she could. My mother told me later that the woman's husband had been a soldier and had brought the spear back from

India where the army had been fighting the heathen savages.

My grandfather, James, also told me that Wolfe and all the other local dogs had had a great time chasing, catching and killing the rats in their Wynd. Having seen the way the dogs in our street had reacted to the invaders, I didn't need much of a description from him. However, even though the Wynds were littered with the bodies of dead rats, I think most of them got away and, from then on, more and more people were finding them inside their houses.

At the same time as the demolition of the Slaughterhouse was taking place, a new Fish Market was being built just where Bridgegate met Clyde Street. My mother thought that this was a great idea because it was much nearer to our house. I agreed with her, remembering all the freezing-cold and rain-soaked Friday detours on the way home from school. I also noticed that men had started building three big pillars in the river which, I was told, were going to be the supports for a bridge which would be bringing a railway across to our side. I thought that this would be exciting as I had never seen a train, but had heard them talked about by my father and my grandas and even Goose who said that he had seen hundreds of them and that they looked like giant dragons.

Eventually, the Laverys came back and I had a great time listening to Goose's stories about all the places they had been and all the things they had done. I noticed that his father had a few more marks on his face and supposed that he had been doing some boxing, as Goose had mentioned that first day at the docks. It was also time for me to go back to school for what would be my last year. Although my hair had grown back and Mrs Lavery's magic potion had kept my head nit-free, I had continued to wear my grandfather's old cap and it now fitted me a lot better. Unfortunately, John Mulgrew thought that it would be great fun to grab it off my head and throw it around the school yard. I didn't think that it was fun at all and punched him on the nose. He didn't think that was funny either and, soon, we were rolling around on the ground accompanied by shouts of "fight, fight, fight" from all the other children in the yard. Needless to say, the noise of the commotion caught the attention of Mother Mary Francis and John and I were dragged into the school by the ear. After receiving a loud and severe telling off we were both given six strokes of the tawse and sent to our class, where we got another telling off from Sister Mary Veronica and were made to stand in separate corners of the classroom for the first hour of the lesson. Although my hands were stinging from the punishment, my thoughts were entirely taken up by my fear that my cap might not be in the yard when I went back for it. As it turned out, my fears were groundless and I was able to recover it when school ended. I didn't say anything to my mother about the fight as she would have been upset and worried after what had happened with the lice, but I was more determined than ever to ask Mr Lavery to teach me to box. I was convinced that, if I learned how to box, nobody would pick on me more than once.

Now that the Laverys were back, my trips to the docks started up again. Every time we went, I learned something new about the different ships, their cargoes and their crews. It was not long before

I found out what Goose meant when he had told me about the Indians and chinks. The Indians were different shades of brown and some of them wore what I thought were bandages on their heads until Mr Lavery told me were called turbans. The chinks or Chinese, to give them their proper name, were a sort of yellow colour and, when they were speaking their funny language, seemed to be singing rather than talking. Mr Lavery told me that the Indians and Chinese worked on British ships and were mostly cooks and laundry boys. It didn't take me long to find out that the other sailors treated them quite badly, including regularly beating them up. I also noticed that the Peelers, when they were about, did nothing to stop these beatings. Sometimes, however, depending on how many people were involved, Mr Lavery would try to stop them. When I asked him about this, he told me that nobody deserved to be treated like that just because of where they came from.

"You know, Willie," he said "our people, the Irish, are treated like that sometimes as well. So don't you be judging people by the colour of their skin or where they come from. There's good and bad everywhere and if a man hasn't done you a bad turn then you shouldn't have anything against him. And don't be afraid to stick up for yourself either, even if it means trouble, because all that will happen is that you'll get picked on again."

I told him about what had happened at school with John Mulgrew and about me wanting to learn how to box.

"Don't you be worrying yourself about the nuns. If you're going to get punished for sticking up for yourself, then make sure that it's worthwhile by leathering the bejasus out of the other fellow so that you won't have to fight him again. I'll teach you how to box alright and a few other things about fighting but I'll tell you the same thing I told Goose. Only fight when you really have to and don't be bullying other people. I also told him that if I catch him picking on other people or bullying them then I'll stick my boot so far up his arse that he'll be choking on the laces and that goes for you too."

I assured him that I wouldn't ever do anything like that and, as the weeks passed, he was true to his word. Every week he would spend half an hour at the side of the cart getting me and Goose to practise the boxing he taught us, as well as getting us to knock lumps out of a sack of straw hanging at the back of the cart. As time went on, he also showed me some other ways to fight, using my head, feet, knees and elbows in addition to my fists. It was during these practice sessions that Goose nicknamed me Winking Willie. Although I wasn't aware of it, I had a habit of blinking my left eye whenever I was punching with my left hand. Mr Lavery thought it was hilarious.

"In this corner, from the Old Wynd we have Winking Willie McCart" he would boom out at least once every time we practised and everyone else, including myself, would fall about laughing.

Mr Lavery also kept his promise of paying me every time I went with them. Most weeks, it would be three pence but, sometimes, he would give me more. One time, he gave me a whole shilling. The hole in the wall was now too small for me to hide my money so I got a small, leather pouch from

Goose, put all my money in it and hid it under a loose floorboard in the house. I really wanted to give some of it to my mother but she would have wanted to know where I got it and I didn't want her to stop me from going with Goose and his family.

All that year, I spent most Saturdays with the Laverys. Sometimes, however, the weather would be so bad that I had to stay at home, but I would be so restless that I would drive my mother mad and she would send me round to my grandfather's house in the Back Wynd so that she could get some peace. It was on one of those occasions that I first heard about the clearances. I had arrived at my grandfather's house to find him and some other men sitting around the table and talking in loud voices. From what I could make out, it seemed that a lot of the houses in the Wynds were going to be knocked down to make way for the new railway that was being built.

"There's no fucking way that they're going to move me and mine out to make way for any fucking railway" said one man that I later learned was Dessie, who had been shouting at my grandfather when Wolfe woke him up.

"But they might not come up as far as your bit" answered another.

"This is just the thin edge of the wedge. I've been hearing about something called the City Improvement Trust, which is supposed to be going to knock down all the houses in all the Wynds and some of King Street, Bridgegate and the Saltmarket as well" my grandfather said.

"And where the fuck are we all supposed to live then, the fucking Green? I'll tell you something. If anybody tries to move me out, they better come ready for trouble because trouble is what they're going to fucking get. My father and a lot of your fathers went through this shite back in Ireland and ended up over here. Well this is one fucking paddy that'll be fighting back" said Dessie, his voice even louder than before.

Everybody else nodded and agreed that they had to make a stand. My grandfather called me over and took me up on his knee.

"It wasn't my father that was driven out it was me. I swore then that I would never go through that again without a fight and I'm not going to. It's not just me and my wife. It's my daughter and this wee one and all the others like them. We've got to stand up for ourselves this time. Even if we get beat, and we probably will, we'll make them think long and hard before they ever do anything like this again."

Although I was caught up in the excitement of the men and their discussion, I was also amazed that the words my grandfather spoke were so similar to the words that Goose's father had used when he had talked about sticking up for myself and making people think twice about picking on me. It was a lesson that I would never forget.

Chapter Thirteen

The Wynds of War

The war in the Wynds began on a Saturday morning, six weeks before Christmas that year. I was standing outside my door waiting for Mrs Lavery to come and get me, when I noticed a large group of Peelers and soldiers coming through the alleyway from the Trongate into the Wynd. They marched past our house down to where the squatters lived. Some of them went into the yards on either side while the rest formed into two lines facing both sides of the buildings. I later found out that other groups had come down New Wynd, Old Wynd, Stockwell Street and King Street.

Suddenly an army officer fired a pistol into the air and with wild shouts, the Peelers and the soldiers ran into the buildings. Unlike previous raids, however, the squatters didn't scatter, as there was nowhere for them to go. A large crowd of mainly women and children from our end of the Wynd had gathered just past the Free Church Mission School to watch what was going on. I could hear shouting and screaming coming from inside the buildings. After a few minutes, soldiers and Peelers came back out dragging women by the hair and throwing them into the middle of the Wynd. Some of the women got up and threw themselves at their attackers. Some of them managed to get in some blows and a few of the attackers found themselves with badly-scratched faces, but the women were very quickly knocked to the ground by clubs and rifle butts. There seemed to be blood everywhere and the Wynd was filled by the sound of moans of pain, crying and shouted curses.

Some of the men who were dragged out fared little better. One man attempted to pull a rifle from the hands of one of the soldiers, but he was struck on the back by another soldier and collapsed on the ground. At this point, other soldiers and Peelers started to kick into him. Some of the women from our end began to shout and tell them to leave the man alone. A Peeler sergeant approached them and told them to shut up and fuck off or they would be next.

Suddenly, there was the sound of a shot being fired and a Peeler came running out of one of the yards holding his arm which had blood pouring from it.

"One of them's got a rifle," he told the sergeant.

"Where the fuck did he get a rifle from?"

"I saw a soldier lying at the other side of the yard. He must have got it off of him."

Soon, I could hear more gunfire and, from the panic on the faces of Peelers and soldiers running out of the buildings, it was plain that the squatters had more than one rifle. Sure enough, from one of the upper glassless windows someone fired a shot which struck the cobbles causing the Peelers and soldiers to scatter for the safety of the yards. We didn't waste any time in heading a safe distance back up the Wynd.

As the morning went on, quite a few injured Peelers and soldiers made their way back up the Wynd to the Trongate accompanied by jeers and catcalls from our neighbours. One woman threw a bucket of piss over the railing as they were passing. A less-injured Peeler ran towards the stairway brandishing his club but he beat a hasty retreat when she brought out a long, bright knife from the folds of her skirt. At the same time, others were herding women, children and a few men from the squatter section into the area in front of the Mission School where they were made to sit down and were put under guard by some soldiers who had, by this time, attached bayonets to the ends of their rifles.

I later found out that the same things were happening in the other Wynds where it was not just the squatters who were under attack. Everybody who lived in the bottom half of the area formed by Stockwell Street, the Trongate, King Street and Bridgegate was to be forced out. My grandfather didn't live in this part, but he still got a beating for helping his pals to fight off the attackers, although he managed to avoid being captured and got back to the safety of his house. Big Dessie wasn't as lucky as he got a bayonet in his back while he was laying into Peelers and soldiers with a leg from his table. He wasn't badly injured, but he wouldn't see his wife and children again for two years, as he would be sentenced to hard labour.

By the time my father came home from work, it was getting dark and the Peelers and soldiers had gone away taking their prisoners with them. My father already knew what had been going on, as word had quickly spread through the city. A few fights had broken out at his work following "Irish papist scum" comments being made by some and reacted to by others

"Mary Ann, you better keep the wee boy away from the school. Until this is sorted out, it won't be safe for you or him to go down that way."

I only realised how worried my father was when he said that he was going down to my grandfather's in Bridgegate after his supper instead of going straight to the pub as he usually did. As it turned out, he did go to the pub after finding out that my grandfather was fine and that his home was safe.

The next day, everyone went off to Mass, as usual. As we passed down the Wynd, we could see and hear makeshift barricades being put up across the entrances to the yards and the buildings. At the chapel, we met my grandmother and grandfather, who could hardly see because of the swelling around his eyes. His whole face seemed to be black and blue from the beating he had been subjected to the day before. I also noticed that he was limping very badly and was hunched over slightly. Everybody was talking about what had happened and the cursing and swearing only stopped when people went in to the chapel itself. When Father McHugh was giving his sermon, he made mention of the events of Saturday and reminded everyone that they had to obey the law. This brought some murmurs from some, which caused him to raise his voice while telling everyone that, according to the Gospel, Jesus had said that the meek would inherit the earth. This didn't seem to go down too well either and even I, at my age, believed that the only the thing that the meek seemed to inherit was a kick in the balls and being treated like scum.

As we were on our way home along Bridgegate, I noticed that there were quite a few handcarts coming out of the New Wynd and the Back Wynd. They were carrying beds, tables, chairs and other small pieces of furniture. There were also people carrying bundles of clothing. Some of the women and children were crying while most of the men walked along silently, staring at the ground. Instead of heading up Old Wynd we carried on along the street, turned in to Back Wynd and walked up towards my grandfather's house. I could see that the people who were leaving were not the squatters who had set up barricades like the ones in our Wynd. My grandfather, who knew most of the people who were leaving, had to stop and sit down on a step halfway up the Wynd as he was shaking quite badly. My grandmother sat beside him and put an arm round his shoulders.

"It's happening again, Lizzie. When are these people going to give us peace and let us live like human beings?"

As he said this, he burst into tears. My mother sat down on his other side and she too was crying as she cuddled into him. I looked at my father who was standing as stiff as a board with a really angry look on his face. I also noticed that his fists were clenched so tightly that his knuckles were white and stood out like two rows of rounded teeth. After a few minutes, my father reached down and helped my grandfather to his feet.

"Come on, James, let's get you home," he said in a soft voice as if he were talking to a child.

After we got my grandfather into the house, we didn't stay very long and, when we went home, we took the long way round along the Trongate in case there was any trouble at the bottom of the Wynds. When we got there, my father joined a group of men who were standing down from our house, while I went up the stairs with my mother to get changed. As I was putting on my old boots, there was a knock on the door and I heard Goose's voice shouting for me. I went out and we both went downstairs and made our way to the alley.

"Fuck me, Willie. Did you see all the fighting yesterday?" he said excitedly.

"Aye and the bastards hurted my granda. See when I'm bigger, Goose, I'm going to find the ones that did it and I'm going to kill them."

"I'm sure they'll all be shiting themselves in case Winking Willie McCart gets them" he laughed.

"It's not funny, Goose. You should see the state he's in."

"I'm not laughing at your granda, Willie. I'm only having a wee joke with you. Come on pal, give us a smile." As he said this he put an arm round my shoulders and pulled me towards him. As I thought about what he had actually said and about how funny it was, I couldn't stop myself from grinning.

"That's better, pal. But don't you worry, Willie. My da said that the time will come when all the people will stand together and all these fuckers in their big fancy houses and palaces will get what's coming to them, and no mistake."

We started to exchange stories about the things we had seen the day before. Goose told me that they had been on their way round to get me, but had been stopped by a road block at the corner of Bridgegate and the Saltmarket. They had carried on down to Clyde Street, but that was closed as well. Turning round they had headed up towards the Trongate. That was a total shambles, so his mother had taken Annie and wee Peter home while Mr Lavery had gone on foot on his own, as he had some stuff to collect from one of the cotton boats and Goose had begun to make his way through the back alleys to come and tell me what had happened. He had got as far as the Back Wynd but, when he saw all the fighting that was going on, he decided to seek some shelter at the top of the stairs of the Free Church and he was stuck there for hours.

"You know, Willie, there's a lot of people who won't be going without a fight."

"But I saw a lot of people leaving this morning." I protested.

"Aye but that's only the ones that are paying rent. My da said that the landlords have offered them other houses to live in over on the other side of the river but, if they don't go today, then they'll get nowhere and they'll get put on the street; so most of them are going. But most folk don't have anywhere to go, so they're putting up a fight. The Peelers and the army will probably be back tomorrow and they'll keep coming back till they've thrown everyone out."

"My granda says that some of the houses in the Saltmarket are getting knocked down as well."

"Aye, that's right. But ours isn't. They're only knocking down the ones between the Trongate and our building. My da says that the railway will be passing right in front of our window so we'll be able to see the trains going past."

All thoughts of the trouble in the Wynds were briefly forgotten as I imagined being able to look out of the window and see a giant dragon passing by.

Chapter Fourteen

Fire Down Below

On the Monday morning, after my father had gone to work, my mother and I went outside and stood by the railing to see what was going to happen, but no Peelers or soldiers appeared. I could see other people standing outside their doors waiting for the trouble to start again. Eventually, some people went back inside while others came down into the Wynd and began talking to each other.

"If it stays quiet you might be able to go to school after all" my mother said

"But my da said I've not to go."

"Aye but that's because he thought that the fighting would start up again. It looks as if that's not going to happen, so you might as well go to school."

As there were still nearly two hours to go until school time, I hoped that, with any luck, the Peelers and soldiers had slept in and would soon be turning up to save me. Unfortunately for me, they didn't turn up and we set off down the Wynd at the usual time to make our way to the school. However, when we reached the bottom it was plain to see that there would be no school for me today. In a change of tactics, the enemy had occupied the deserted houses at the bottom of the New Wynd and were using them as a base from which to attack the still-occupied buildings. This time, however, they were only targeting one or two buildings at a time and seemed to be being very successful, judging by the numbers of people who were being escorted into Bridgegate and herded over to the land that was being used to build the new Fish Market. I noticed that the men and older boys were taken down to the riverside and put on to a big three-masted boat that was tied up a little bit downstream from the railway pillars.

All thoughts of school now gone, we turned back and headed home. As we walked up the Wynd, we passed old Mr Hennessy, who only had one leg and who was sitting in a chair outside his door. My mother told him what was happening and he said that they would probably come through the back yards and attack Old Wynd and Back Wynd from behind to avoid the barricades.

If this had been the plan, it would probably have worked, given the success of the New Wynd action. However, something went wrong. Although there were many opinions about who was to blame, nobody knows, for certain, who, or what started the fire. Early in the afternoon, we could hear shouting and the odd gunshot coming from the bottom end of our Wynd but nothing compared to Saturday. Very soon, however, thick smoke was being blown by the wind off the river up towards where we lived. Soon it became possible to see that some buildings on the left of the bottom of the Wynd were on fire. Since none of the windows down there had glass in them, flames could be seen reaching out and licking their way up to the floors above. A lot of people, including my mother and I, went down for a closer look and wished that we hadn't. There were people trapped above the flames and they were screaming for help but those people who did try to get in to help them couldn't get past the barricades that had been put up to stop the Peelers. Children were dropped into the arms of people below. Not all of them were caught safely and some were badly hurt when they landed on the cobbles instead. Some of the adults were also injured when they hit the ground and the noise of the flames, the crackle of burning timber and the screams of the trapped were joined by the screams of pain of the injured and the crying of the women bystanders, who felt almost powerless to help.

Very soon, even that limited help became impossible to deliver. Burning embers had been blown across the narrow gap and through the glassless windows of the buildings at the other side of the Wynd where they, very soon, set alight the hessian sacks which had been put up as window coverings. Luckily, the people at that side had enough time to break down the barricades and escape to safety. Soon, both sides of the Wynd were ablaze and everybody moved well away from the danger. From what I could hear from the talk among the adults, the fires seemed to be taking hold of the buildings at the bottom of all the Wynds and that, if the wind kept blowing up from the river, would soon be heading up towards us. It was evident that this was a real danger as more and more of the squatter people, coughing and spluttering, their faces and clothes blackened by the smoke, were making their way up towards the alley at the top of the Wynd and out into the Trongate.

Suddenly, there were cries of fear and some people came running back into the Wynd. Behind them came a large group of soldiers, with bayonets on their rifles, who formed a line on either side of, what must have been about twenty, handcarts carrying four big barrels each. The soldiers ignored the squatters and they and the handcarts made their way down towards the burning buildings. At about the halfway point the handcarts were pushed into the yards at either side of the Wynd. After about half an hour, the men who had been pushing the carts came back up and stood in a group smoking and talking amongst themselves. I could hear shouting coming from further down but, with all the other noise going on, nobody seemed to be able to make out what the shouting was about. One of the women asked a handcart man what was happening and he told her that the soldiers were giving everybody down that end a final warning before the buildings were blown up to prevent the fire from spreading.

About five minutes later, the soldiers came back up. A sergeant counted how many men were there and, when satisfied, reported to the officer who was in charge, who then ordered that the fuses be lit. Two soldiers ran back down and returned very quickly, saluted the officer and informed him that his orders had been carried out. It seemed that it was only seconds later that I heard what seemed like a whole series of loud explosions followed by the noise of falling buildings. Before long, the smoke being blown towards us was thickened by choking dust and everyone, including the soldiers, ran either indoors or up and out through the alley. I later learned that the same thing had happened from King Street to Stockwell Street, even where the fires hadn't yet taken hold. Nobody attempted to put the fires out and all the bottom buildings were left to burn. One way or another, the war was over and the people were gone.

Although nobody could prove or disprove it, I heard my father saying to my mother that he was sure that it had been the authorities who caused the fire and that it was impossible that the powder that had been used to blow up the buildings could have been transported from the arsenal to the Wynds in such a short time from the outbreak of the fire.

While I tend to side with my father's opinion about who started the fire, what no-one knows, for sure, are the numbers of people who died or were badly injured as a result of the fire, of falling to the street, or by being trapped and killed inside the blown-up buildings.

The next day, my mother got me ready for school, but we couldn't go our usual way because the buildings were still smouldering at the bottom of the Wynd. Instead, we went up into the Trongate and made our way along to the Saltmarket. I could see that many of the squatters must have slept in the street during the night as there were small groups of mainly women and children, many with still-blackened faces streaked with tears, sitting against the walls of the buildings all along the street. I asked my mother what was going to happen to them. She replied that she didn't know but that they would probably have to find somewhere else to squat or, more likely, they would have to go to the Poorhouse.

I later found that nearly all of the men and older boys, who had been taken to the ship on the river, were charged and convicted of rioting, assault, malicious wounding and affray. Some of them were sentenced to hard labour but most were part of the last group to be transported to Australia, some for at least ten years and others for life. So my mother was probably right. Without their men to provide for them, whole families were destitute and would have no choice but to go into the Poorhouse.

Strangely, whilst people had once looked down on and had nothing good to say about the squatters, the actions of the Peelers, soldiers and people controlling them caused a great deal of anger amongst the remaining population. My own feeling was that what Goose had said about people standing together was all well and good but, unless they were also prepared to be as ruthless as the other side, then they would have no chance and would probably end up losing, just like the squatters had lost. This had been a lesson which would mean more to me than any of the lessons learned in all my time at school.

Chapter Fifteen

Death and Waxy's

Within a couple of weeks, all the buildings at the bottom had been demolished and cleared and a fence was built from Stockwell Street, along Goosedubs and Bridgegate to King Street. This meant that everyone had to use the Trongate to get out of the Wynds, although we could still get through the backyards into the other Wynds, King Street and Stockwell Street.

When Goose and his mother came to get me on the Saturday, we had to use the backyards, and then walk down to the bottom of Stockwell Street to meet up with Mr Lavery and the rest of the family. Although the slaughterhouse was now gone, Clyde Street seemed to be busier than usual. I asked Mr Lavery why this was.

"You'll see when we get to Jamaica Street, Willie. They've started to lay tramlines from Eglinton Street up to Maryhill."

"Who's Mary Hill and what are tramlines?" I asked.

"No, Willie, it's not Mary Hill, it's a place called Maryhill which is a few miles up that way," he said with a laugh and pointed over to his right. "And tramlines are for the new tramcars to run on. See that omnibus over there, well tramcars are just like those, but they have wheels like trains and they are pulled along on rails."

"But why do we need tramcars if we've already got omnibuses?"

"That's a question that me and a lot of other people have been asking and, to be quite truthful, I don't know the answer but I'll bet there's money involved for somebody."

When we reached Jamaica Street, it took us nearly ten minutes to get across. Everyone who was driving a cart, omnibus or pushing a handcart was shouting and swearing at one another to get out of the way. And everyone, including people on foot, was giving pelters to the men who were working in the road. There were a few fistfights as people reacted to the cursing and name-calling but we did get across safely without getting involved and we went about our usual business.

We left for home a little earlier than usual because it was going to takes us a bit longer to get back. Mr Lavery dropped off Goose, his mother and me at Stockwell Street. When we got to my house, we were surprised to find that my mother wasn't there, although the door wasn't locked. When we walked back outside to the top of the stairs, I heard Mrs McGhee shouting from across the street.

"Willie, son, your ma had to go to your granda's about an hour ago. I think he's not well. She asked me to tell you and your da to go over there when youse came home."

"Thanks, Mrs McGhee." I replied, a little confused.

"Where does your granda stay, Willie?" Mrs Lavery asked.

"Over in Back Wynd. Do you think my granda will be alright?"

"I'm sure he will be. Come on I'll take you over there. You can show me the way." As she said this, she took me by the hand and we walked up to the alley. We walked along till we reached the top of Back Wynd. Mrs Lavery told Goose to carry on home and tell his father that she would be a little bit late.

"Right ma. I'll see you tomorrow, Willie, and I hope your granda's all right." He gave us both a wave and headed off along the street.

However, when we reached my grandfather's house it was obvious that my grandfather wasn't all right. Even from the bottom of the stairs, I could hear people crying.

"You best wait here, Willie" said Mrs Lavery in a voice even softer than usual.

I didn't object as I dreaded finding out the reason for all the crying. Mrs Lavery went up to the top of the stairs and knocked on the door. As the door was opened to let her in, the sound of the crying got louder. While I waited, I slowly made my way to the top of the stairs. Just as I reached the top, the door opened again and I saw Father McHugh standing there with a purple cloth over his shoulders and a prayer book in his hand. He sat down on the top step and motioned for me to sit beside him.

"Willie, your mother has asked me to come and tell you about your grandfather."

"Is he dead?" I asked, surprised by my own willingness to believe the worst.

"Yes. Your grandfather has gone to heaven to be with the angels. I can assure you that he is with them right now because he made his peace with God before he went."

"Will he be with Mary Ann?" I sobbed, tears streaming down my face.

"Yes. And with your big sister, Lizzie too. He'll be telling them all about you. How you are a brave boy and how you will be helping your mother in this very sad time for her. You are a brave boy aren't you, Willie?"

"Y-y-yes, Father," I replied feeling anything but brave and wishing that my mother had her arms around me and was telling me to wake up as I was having a bad dream.

"That's a good boy. Now I want you to go in and see your mother and your grandmother and be as brave as you can. Will you do that for me?"

"Y-y-yes, Father" I replied as I got up and went into the house.

All thoughts of being brave disappeared when my mother, still crying, saw me and ran and picked me up, squeezing me so tightly that it hurt. Seeing her tears, it was impossible for me not to start crying but when I did, I did it in silence. My grandmother was sitting on the edge of the bed holding the palm of my grandfather's left hand in the palm of her left. With her right hand she was stroking his forehead. To me, it looked as if he was sleeping and that I wouldn't be surprised if he woke up and asked what all the noise was about.

My mother sat me down in my grandfather's chair and, after thanking Goose's mother for bringing me round, asked her if she would like some tea. Mrs Lavery thanked her but said that she would have to be going home. While this conversation was going on, I looked over at my grandmother. She saw me looking and, although the tears were still streaming down her cheeks, she gave me a little smile. For some reason, I don't know what, I suddenly felt as if I wasn't so sad anymore and I got up and went over to her. She let go of my grandfather and wrapped her arms around me, hugging me tightly to her chest. However, having got nearer to my grandfather, I could see that he still had the marks of the beating he had received. My eyes filled with tears, once again, and I started to tremble.

"There, there, Willie. Your granda wouldn't want to be seeing you cry. He would want you to be happy for him because he's gone to heaven. You know your granda always liked to make you happy"

I tried to nod but couldn't because she had pulled my head back against her chest. What she couldn't know was that my tears and my trembling were not wholly caused by sadness. They were caused more through anger at what had been done to him for standing up for what he thought was right and also a little anger at myself that I had not been old enough, or big enough, to be there to help him. However, I was more determined than ever that I would get the ones who had done this and that if, when I was older, I was ever involved in anything like this then it would be the other lot that would be getting beaten up or killed, not me.

Not long after Mrs Lavery had left, my father came in. He went over to my mother and squeezed her shoulder then told my grandmother how sorry he was that my grandfather had died and asked her what had happened. My grandmother thanked him and told him that he had suddenly started to cough up blood and that it had just kept coming until he passed out. After that, he had never woken up again and she had asked her neighbour to go to my mother and to ask her to get the priest. Father McHugh had come and had just finished giving him the last sacraments when he died. My father muttered what sounded like "murdering bastards" and he came over to me and nodded his head to tell me to get up and let him sit down in my grandfather's chair. I moved over to the table and sat beside my mother who was pouring some tea into a cup for him.

"Mary Ann, there's a wee drop of stew and potatoes in the pot that you can heat up and give to James. I'm sure he'll be starving with him just coming in from his work."

As my grandmother said this, I saw a look of shock on my mother's face.

"Oh no!" she cried "I left in such a hurry that I left James' dinner on the stove. It will be boiled away to nothing."

"Don't worry," said my father. "I took it off before I came round. But I left the pots for the bath on so they'll be ready when we get home."

This must have been my father's way of letting her know that he wouldn't be staying long and that he expected her to be going home with him and not staying with my grandmother.

"It might be better, Mary Ann, if you go home and give James his supper. If you want, I'll keep Willie here and give him something to eat and you can maybe come round and take him home later. It would be good company for me as well."

My mother didn't say anything but my father got up without drinking his tea, said a mumbled goodbye to my grandmother and went out. My mother went over and gave my grandmother a hug, kissed me on the forehead and told me that she would come back round later before following my father out the door.

While I was eating my supper, my grandmother told me all about how she had first met my grandfather and about all the hard times they had gone through when they were living in Ireland. She was telling me about how they had had to walk nearly sixty miles from the small cottage that they lived in to get to Belfast so that they could get the boat to Glasgow, when there was a knock on the door. She went to open the door and, although I could not see who was there, I recognized the voice right away. It was Mr Lavery.

"Good evening to you, Mrs Toner. My name is Ben Lavery. My wife brought young Willie round earlier and she came home and told me of your sad loss. I wonder if I might come in and pay my respects to James."

"But of course," my grandmother replied showing him in to the middle of the room.

"You all right there, Willie?" he asked as he saw me sitting at the table.

"Yes, thanks Mr Lavery," I replied and for some strange reason, I felt tears in my eyes again.

"Did you know my granda, Mr Lavery?" I asked in astonishment.

"Sure I've known James for years. In fact we had a drink together a couple of weeks ago. It breaks my heart to see him ending up like this because he was a great man, so he was."

After he said this he leaned over and kissed my grandfather on the forehead.

"Would you like a cup of tea Mr Lavery?

"Please, call me Ben and, if you don't mind what I would like to do is to borrow young Willie here for ten or fifteen minutes to help me with a little errand."

Before she could answer, the door opened and my mother walked in. I could see that she was wondering who this man was who was in her mother's house.

"Mammy, this is Goose's da, Mr Lavery."

"Oh, very pleased to meet you Mr Lavery," she said as she smiled and reached out to shake his hand.

"And you Mrs McCart. Please accept my deepest condolences for your sad loss. If there's anything I can do to help, you only have to ask."

"Thank you very much" she said as she sat down, her face, once again, sad and drawn.

"I was just asking your ma if it would be all right for young Willie to come and give me a hand with a small errand for ten or fifteen minutes. I'll bring him straight back."

"As long as he's not away any longer as it's getting really dark outside and you never know what could happen with all the bother there's been already this week."

"Right come on then, Willie," he said as he went out the door.

When we got to the bottom of the stairs, he told me to wait. He went into a corner of the yard and came back with two sacks. I could hear the clinking of the contents of the sacks.

"Is that the poteen?" I asked.

"Sh! Not so loud. Aye it's poteen and I'm taking it over to Waxy Mulligan's."

Waxy Mulligan's shebeen was about halfway between my grandfather's house and the back door of the Britannia Music Hall. I knew where it was, but I had never been there. I knew that it wasn't a place for children, so I wondered why Mr Lavery needed me to go with him. To get to Waxy's we had to go through a close. There was a man at each end of the close. Before we could go into the close, the man who was there held up a lantern so that he could see Mr Lavery's face. At the same time the light showed his face and I was just a little frightened when I saw that he had a deep scar, which seemed to start at his hairline and run down across his left eye to his chin, just missing his mouth.

"Ah. It's yourself, Ben. And who's this?"

110

"It's me alright, Martin, and this is young Willie McCart. He's James Toner's grandson. I'm taking him in to see Waxy."

"Ah, poor James. I'm sorry for your loss, son" he said as he crossed himself with his free hand.

We walked through the close and past the man at the other end. We then went up a flight of stairs and Mr Lavery knocked on the door at the top. A man's face appeared at the small glass window above the door, then disappeared again. The door opened and I was astonished by the noises that came out. As well as the sound of numerous voices talking, there were at least three different songs being sung. In spite of there being a lot of lanterns and candles, I could hardly see anything because of all the smoke. There was a short, narrow lobby leading to, what seemed like, a large room at the end but we did not go there. Instead, Mr Lavery turned to his right and I saw a door that I hadn't noticed before. Mr Lavery told the man whose face I had seen above the door that he had business with Waxy, knocked on the door and went in, motioning for me to follow him.

On the other side of the door was a small room with a table and four wooden chairs and nothing else apart from a fireplace which had no fire lit in it.

"Evening, Waxy. I've got your usual. I've also brought young Willie here. Willie is James Toner's grandson and I was thinking that you might be willing to help out the family of a fellow Ribbonman at this terrible time."

"I take it that you're thinking about the wake then, Lavery, you sly fucker that you are."

"To be sure, Waxy, aren't you the one for trying to put words in my mouth. I never mentioned such a thing. Willie, did you hear me mention the wake?"

I just shook my head. Fascinated by the conversation and wondering what a Ribbonman was.

"Anyway. It doesn't matter. James was a good friend and comrade as well as a good customer. I'll tell you what," Waxy said, looking at me "You go back and tell your granny that Waxy Mulligan will be along tomorrow after Mass to see her and that she'll not need to worry about the wake. I'll take care of that. Oh and you can also tell her that Ben Lavery here has offered the services of his horse and cart for the funeral." As he said this he slapped Mr Lavery on the back and gave a hearty laugh.

When we returned, Mr Lavery told my grandmother what Waxy had said and confirmed that we would be able to use his horse and cart for my grandfather's funeral. Both my mother and my grandmother started crying again but they thanked Mr Lavery for all his help at least three times before he left for home.

Chapter Sixteen

Wolfe Toner

The next morning, we all went off to Mass, as usual, although we had to go the long way round through backyards and closes because of the fence at the bottom of the Wynd. I was surprised to see that my grandmother wasn't there but my mother told me that it was not proper for my grandfather to be left alone in the house and that my grandmother would be going to a later Mass in St Alphonsus' chapel, which was just up the road from my school. During the Mass, Father McHugh told everyone that my grandfather had died and that his funeral would take place on Wednesday. He also asked everyone to pray for the repose of my grandfather's soul and for all his family and friends. After Mass, lots of people came up to my mother and father and told them how sorry they were that my grandfather had died. Many of the men who spoke to them accompanied their condolences with remarks about the circumstances of his death and their fervent wishes that those responsible would burn in hell.

Instead of going home, we carried on to my grandfather's house, where we found my grandmother sitting with Waxy Mulligan and three other men including the big man with the scar who had been guarding the close on the previous night. There were also two women there, whom I didn't know. About five minutes after we went in, my father and all the men got up and went outside and I was left with the women.

"What about Liam?" one of the women asked my grandmother.

"I don't know how to get in touch with him and I don't know if he would even come anyway," my grandmother replied choking back a sob.

My uncle Liam was my mother's brother and he had got married to a Protestant woman in a Protestant church in Hawick, Roxburghshire when I was two years old. This had led to a major fall-out with my grandfather which, when a mixed marriage was involved, was quite commonplace at the time. My uncle Liam had never come back home after that and neither I nor the rest of the family had ever seen him since. Although we knew that he had two boys, my cousins, we hadn't met them either.

When it came time for my grandmother to go to Mass, she asked me if I would like to go with her. Normally, the idea of going to Mass twice in one day would not have appealed to me in the slightest, but I didn't think twice about saying that I would.

"Mind, Willie, you've already been to communion so you can't go again" my mother warned me.

"I know, mammy." I replied, surprised that she felt that she had to remind me when this was one of the rules that had been drummed into me when I was preparing for my First Communion.

As we came out of the alley into the Trongate, my grandmother took my hand as we walked along. Unlike other days, there was very little traffic on the street, although there were quite a few people walking about. From the way most of them were dressed, I could tell that they were not from the Wynds. The men wore smart suits of clothes and all manner of hats, not caps, and the women all seemed to be wearing similarly smart dresses and coats. I noticed that many of the women, and a few of the men, held handkerchiefs to their mouths and walked faster when they passed the entrances to the Wynds.

"Why are they covering their mouths, granny?"

"They don't like the smell."

"Doesn't it smell where they live?" I asked. I was puzzled because, at that time of my life, it seemed to me that everywhere I went had smells. There was the fish smell on the way to school, the stink of the Wynds and a lot of unrecognizable smells around the docks.

"It probably does but maybe it's a nicer smell."

"And is that why they walk faster as well?"

This question brought a small laugh from my grandmother.

"No, Willie. They walk faster because they are scared that an Irishman will jump out at them and put a plaster over their mouths, smother them and drag   them   away."
Seeing my look of puzzlement, she explained.

"A few years ago, two Irishmen in Edinburgh were hanged for robbing graves and killing people so that they could sell their bodies. Ever since that time, many people have been scared that this would happen to them, so they hurry past anywhere that has lots of Irish people living there. Your granda used to

115

say that he found it strange that people were scared of the Irish but weren't scared of Scottish doctors, when it was a Scottish doctor who had been buying the bodies."

I, once again, marvelled at my grandfather's wisdom but, in my child-mind, I was also glad that Edinburgh was so far away from my sisters, and my grandfather, for that matter.

After we had crossed King Street, we moved along towards Glasgow Cross and the top of the Saltmarket. As we passed the statue of a man on a horse, my grandmother spat on the road and made the sign of the cross.

"What's wrong granny?"

She pointed to the statue and told me that it was a statue of King William who had been bad to the Catholics in Ireland. It was, in fact, a statue of King William III, the Prince of Orange. He was married to Mary Stewart, the sister of King James II and had been persuaded to lead the Glorious Revolution of 1688, which would maintain the Protestant Ascendancy in the United Kingdom. This revolution had culminated in the Battle of the Boyne in Ireland in 1690, where the mainly Catholic Irish army of King James had been defeated. William's campaign had been funded by London merchants who foresaw the benefits of a sovereign link between the House of Orange and the United Kingdom. Such a link provided easy access to the expertise of the Dutch East India Company, which dominated European trade with Asia at that time. Of course the majority of people fighting on both sides believed that they were fighting a religious war and knew nothing of the financial elements involved. This would not be the last time that such a cruel deception would be perpetrated upon common people, not least on the island of Ireland.

It took us another twenty minutes or so until we reached St Alphonsus'. I had been there a few times before with the nuns but it seemed different, somehow more pleasant, because I was with my grandmother. Nobody mentioned my grandfather during the Mass.

After Mass, we retraced our steps towards home.

"Willie, could you do your granny a big favour?"

"Aye," I replied more than willing to do anything for her.

"I need someone to look after wee Wolfe until after your granda's funeral, as there are going to be a lot of people coming and going and I won't have time to look after him."

I had completely forgotten about Wolfe. I then remembered that he had been in the house all the time, but had been curled up in the corner over by the sink. I hadn't even thought it strange that he hadn't been jumping about excitedly, as he usually did when we went into my grandfather's house.

"Is Wolfe sad too?" I asked with childish innocence.

"I dare say that he is, but I'm sure that he would cheer up a bit if he was with you for a wee while." She replied with a smile.

"Do you think I should ask my da if it will be alright for Wolfe to stay with us?"

"I'll get your ma to ask him for you. She'll pick the right time to ask him."

Even I knew that the right time to ask him would be after he had had a couple of drinks and was still in a good mood.

The thought of being able to play with Wolfe, even for just a few days, cheered me up no end and it seemed like no time at all before we were back at the house. My father, Waxy Mulligan and quite a few other men were standing at the bottom of the stairs smoking and drinking from bottles. I was surprised that they all seemed to be laughing and joking even though my grandfather was lying dead up in the house. This was my first experience of an Irish wake. A time of sadness at the passing of a loved one was accompanied by a celebration. Originally, this was to celebrate the passing of the deceased to a better life in heaven, but had evolved into a sort of party where the deceased was the honoured guest and where stories, mostly of a humorous nature, were exchanged, not only about the person who had died, but about others who had gone before.

Just as we were going through the door, my grandfather, Willie, was coming out. He put his arms around my grandmother and held her tightly.

"Lizzie, I'm sure sorry for your sad loss. It's a sad day for us all, and no mistake, when a fine gentleman like himself is taken from us."

"Thanks very much, Willie, you're very kind." She replied softly.

"And you, lad. Are you keeping your chin up and being brave for your ma and your granny?"

I nodded but my mind was racing and I was confused by why everyone, from Father McHugh to my grandfather, wanted me to be brave. I didn't want to be brave. "Did they not realise that I wanted to cry and cry because my grandfather was dead? Did they not realise that I was still a wee boy and that it would be years and years before I died and I would be able see him again in heaven? If they wanted me to be brave then I would try to be brave but when I was alone I would cry if I wanted to!"

Inside the house, the table was covered with different types of food and a lot of women were standing around talking. I couldn't understand how so many people could fit into such a small space. There seemed to be so many different conversations going on at the same time. I noticed that my auntie Hannah was sitting on one of the chairs but didn't seem to be talking to anyone. As usual, her face was grim and was probably the only face in the room that would have given any unsuspecting visitor a clue that there had been a recent death. When I managed to get through the crowd and reach the bed, I noticed that my grandfather had been dressed in his Sunday suit and tie and that his face was clean and his hair combed. Even the bruises on his face were almost invisible and I, once again, thought and hoped that he would wake up. While standing at the bedside, I felt something touching my leg. When I looked down I saw Wolfe's head protruding from underneath the bed. I crouched down and he came out and nestled between my thighs. As I patted him softly and looked into his eyes, which seemed so much wider than I ever remembered, I was convinced that he knew that my grandfather had gone too. I wondered to myself if dogs could cry and

119

if they also went to heaven when *they* died. I thought that maybe they had a different heaven from us and poor wee Wolfe wouldn't see my grandfather again. I decided that, when I got the chance, I would tell Wolfe about heaven and that, even though I didn't know for sure, when *he* died he would see my grandfather again.

I asked my mother if I could take Wolfe out for a walk. I didn't feel very comfortable with so many people in such a small space and nobody was talking to me anyway. She told me not to go far and to make sure that I kept a tight hold of the rope so that he didn't run away. She needn't have worried. After we got downstairs and through the crowd of men at the bottom, we set off through the yards. I had decided to go over to my own house in case Goose had come looking for me. Although I saw a lot more rats than usual because of all the demolitions that had taken place, not once did Wolfe make any attempt to go after them or even let out a yelp.

When we reached my house in Old Wynd, there was no sign of Goose. I decided to wait and see if he turned up and, all the while, Wolfe just sat on the step beside me. I told him all I thought I knew about heaven.

"When you go to heaven, Wolfe, you'll see my granda again. There will be lots of rats for you to chase and you can bark as much as you like because nobody will complain. And there'll be lots of good stuff to eat. Every day will be sunny and warm and it will never rain. There'll be lots of angels singing and everybody will be able to look up and see God smiling at them."

120

I went on in this vein for quite a while, detailing more and more about all the good stuff that there would be in heaven, but Wolfe just continued to sit still not even looking at me when I was speaking. Eventually, I ran out of imagination and just sat there in silence beside the wee dog.

After a while, as it was starting to get dark, I decided that Goose wouldn't be coming and that I had better start making my way back to my grandfather's house. Just as I was ready to turn into the yard leading to New Wynd, my mother came walking through.

"I thought this is where you would be. We were getting a bit worried since you were away so long. Come on, son, it's time to go home."

"But, mammy, I'll need to take Wolfe home."

"There's no need. I've spoken to your da and he says it's all right for him to stay with us for a while."

Obviously, my mother had picked the right time to ask him and I was more than happy that she had. I was also glad that my grandmother had given her some food to take home. I hadn't had anything to eat since Saturday night. Usually, we had something after the Mass because of the three-hour fast but, because we hadn't gone home and because of everything else that was happening, I had forgotten about my stomach. When we got into the house I wasted no time in bolting down bread, cheese and some dried meat. I ate it so fast that I brought on a fit of the hiccups."

"See! That's what happens when you act like a greedy guts!" my mother scolded me. She filled a cup with previously-boiled water from a pot on the range and told me to drink it all down while holding my nose to stop the hiccups. I did as she told me, but it didn't work and it was about another five minutes before they stopped.

My mother put a bit of the dried meat and some water down for Wolfe, but he didn't even sniff at it. Instead, he curled up in front of my father's chair.

Later, as I was in bed, my mother woke me up. In the dim light, I could see that she had her forefinger in front of her mouth indicating that I should be quiet.

"Listen, Willie," she whispered.

I could hear my father, obviously drunk, talking to someone and I lifted my head above my mother's shoulder to see who it was. My father was sitting in his chair and Wolfe was sitting at his feet and looking up at him.

"Wolfe is it? Fuck me I've just realised it's Wolfe Toner. By Christ that James Toner never missed a trick. Wolfe Toner! Well, Wolfe Toner, if you're going to be living under my roof then you'll have to earn your keep. If I see as much as a rat's tail in this house then you'll be out on your arse. Do you understand?"

Wolfe just sat there looking at him as he continued to ramble on until he fell asleep on the chair. My mother and I lay awake for a while shaking silently with laughter at the one-sided conversation we had been witness to.

The next morning we were awakened by a shout from my father.

"What the fuck! Mary Ann look what the dog's done."

I was afraid that maybe Wolfe had pissed or even worse, shat on the floor and of what my father might do to him. However, when I looked over, I could see that my father was still sitting in his chair where he had slept and there, between his feet, sat Wolfe with the body of a dead rat in his mouth.

"Well you did tell him last night that he had to earn his keep," my mother laughed as she got out of bed. "And it looks like he's done just that, wouldn't you say?"

"Did I? Well if I did then it's plain that that is one clever fucker of a dog, and no mistake. Imagine that! Wait till I tell everyone at work about this. Nobody will believe it."

I think that that must have been the only morning that I remember my father leaving for his work with a smile on his face.

Chapter Seventeen

The Wearin o' the Green

Because Mr Lavery was going to provide his cart to take my grandfather to the graveyard, my grandmother was able to save a little bit of money from the penny-policy insurance, as all she had to pay for was the coffin and the cemetery fees, plus a donation to the chapel. As far as I know, all the drink for the wake was provided by Waxy Mulligan, free of charge, and all the food was provided by the neighbours. In addition, there had been a small collection locally and this money was also given to my grandmother. Thinking back, this must have seemed like a godsend since she had now lost the money coming in from my grandfather's work.

The night before the funeral, my grandfather's body had to be taken to the chapel. By this time, he had been put in a coffin and everyone had the chance to say goodbye and then go outside while the lid was put on. As I stood at the door, I could hear a heated conversation taking place at the bottom of the stairs where my father, Waxy Mulligan and a few other men were standing.

"Tuberculosis my fucking arse," I heard Waxy Mulligan almost shout.

"Well that's what that bastard of a doctor put on the certificate. He said that coughing up blood was a sure sign of the presence of tuberculosis." I heard my father reply

"Being kicked in the guts by half a dozen Peeler boots is why he was coughing up blood. Sure James never had a day's illness in all the time I knew him. Even at his age, he was as fit as you or I. Tuberculosis? Doctors? A bunch of fucking charlatans, that's what they are and..."

Before Waxy could continue, someone tapped him on the arm and nodded towards the house from where the coffin was being brought out. It had been decided that the coffin would be carried all the way to the chapel rather than taken on the cart. Around six o' clock in the evening, the coffin was carried downstairs and put on the shoulders of six men one of whom was my father. Because of the closure of the bottom of the Wynd, the coffin, and the many people who were walking behind, had to pass through the alley and into the Trongate. From there, the procession made its way along the Trongate, down Stockwell Street and along Clyde Street to the chapel. On the way, other men took over the carrying of the coffin. This happened twice in all. I remember that the rain fell constantly and I was glad, since that meant that the tears that I was shedding were disguised by the water running down my face. Unusually, I wasn't wearing my cap, as my mother had said that it would be disrespectful to wear a cap during a funeral procession.

When we reached the chapel, Father McHugh was waiting at the doors with two altar boys. He turned and led the procession into the chapel, while saying prayers welcoming my grandfather to spend his last night of rest before his funeral the next day. The

125

coffin was placed on a wooden stand in front of the altar gates. Four large candles on massive brass candlesticks were lit and placed at the head, foot and either side of the coffin to symbolise a crucifix. The coffin, itself, was covered with a large black cloth, and a small crucifix and a book of the Gospels were placed on top. After a few more prayers, the ceremony was ended but a lot of people stayed behind to go to confession in preparation for the Mass the next day. As I was leaving with my mother and my grandmother, I saw Mrs Lavery with Goose, Annie and wee Peter. I knew that Mr Lavery was there, too, since he had been one of the men carrying the coffin. When we were all outside, Mrs Lavery came over and hugged my mother and my grandmother. Annie gave me a hug and Goose gave me an awkward handshake.

"I'm sorry about your granda, Willie," he sort of stuttered and I was surprised to see that he had tears in his eyes. I think that this was the first time that I ever thought of the Laverys, and of Goose, in particular, as being more than just friends. Even at my young age, I recognised that these were people who were sharing my pain more like relatives than friends.

When we reached the top of Back Wynd, Mrs Lavery and her family carried on along the Trongate while the rest of us went down to my grandmother's house. We didn't stay very long as it was already dark. I had left Wolfe at my grandmother's house but she told me to take him with me when my mother and I left for home. It was some hours later before my father came home. Although we were already in bed, we weren't asleep and it was obvious that he had had a few drinks again.

On the Wednesday, before the funeral Mass started, as I was sitting in the front row with my grandmother and my mother and father, a man came walking down the centre aisle and round to the front of where we were seated.

"Hello, mammy," he said.

My grandmother stood up and hugged him, tears streaming down her face.

"Oh, Liam, son. I didn't know how to find you and tell you about your da," she sobbed.

"It's all right mammy, I'm here now."

My mother was also on her feet and she gave him a big hug too before my grandmother told him to come and sit beside her.

"I've left Lizzie up the back with the wee ones."

"Well go and bring them down then. The whole family should be together for once."

He went away and returned with my auntie Lizzie and my two wee cousins, James and William. I noticed that they seemed a bit uncomfortable at first. This was understandable since it was the first time that they had met my grandmother and the family and we would have been total strangers to them. In addition, at that time, it was extremely uncommon for non-Catholics to set foot inside a chapel unless it was for criminal purposes. I am ashamed to admit that I don't remember a lot about the actual Mass as I was too busy looking at my newly-found relatives. What I do remember, however, was some of the eulogy given to my grandfather by Father McHugh, who was dressed in vestments as black as the pall covering the coffin.

"James Toner was born in Fermanagh in 1813. He was the only son of James Toner and Fanny Dorrity. Shortly after his marriage to Elizabeth King and the birth of his son, William who, I am glad to say, is with his mother today to join with us in saying goodbye as we commit James to the care of Our Lord Jesus Christ and Mary, his mother. He had to leave Ireland because of the famine, believing and hoping that he would find a better life for himself and his family over here in Glasgow. However, as you well know, like most of the others who came here, he found that it was far from easy for an Irishman to make a decent living or to be afforded respect in this city. Despite these difficulties, however, through his sweat and toil, he carved out a living for his family, which now included his daughter, Mary Ann. I have no doubt that James Toner is today in the arms of the Lord. This was a man who, through thick and thin, remained true to his faith and who left this earth secured by the grace of God. In our prayers today, let us remember the soul of James Toner and let us also remember to pray for all his family and friends that they might be consoled in their grief at the loss of such a well-loved husband, father, grandfather and friend. Also, on behalf of James' family, I would like to thank you all for turning out in such great numbers as a magnificent demonstration of the sure respect in which you held their loved-one."

It was, indeed, a tremendous turn-out for my grandfather, because most of the men would have had to sacrifice a day's wages to attend his funeral and that was no small matter when they were already working for a bare pittance.

When the Mass was over, the coffin was sprinkled with Holy Water and censed with incense as a symbol of prayers rising to heaven. Before the coffin was lifted, one of the men who had carried it in came over to my uncle Liam and suggested that he take his place in carrying it out of the chapel. My grandmother gave Uncle Liam a pleading look and he got up and made his way to the front. The coffin was lifted, turned around and hoisted on to the shoulders of the pall bearers. I noticed that four of the pall bearers, like many other men present, were wearing a small, green rosette in the lapel of their jackets. The green rosette was the symbol of members of the Ribbon Society. This was an organisation which had been founded in rural parts of Ireland as a defence against attacks by Orangemen following the failure of the uprising, inspired by the French Revolution and led by the United Society of Irishmen, paradoxically a mainly liberal-Protestant organisation, in 1798. Some of its members had come over to settle in Glasgow and other areas of Britain and had kept the organisation going by recruiting new members from within the Irish communities. Generally, most of its members treated the organisation as a sort of Irish club, but quite a few played an active role in the activities of the Fenian Brotherhood, who were intent on gaining Home Rule for Ireland. The Orange Order had also developed in many areas of Scotland and England. Introduced, primarily, by returning soldiers who had served alongside the Orange Yeomanry in the quelling of the 1798 uprising and mainly regiment-

129

based, membership subsequently spread to the Protestant civilian population in response to the perceived growth of Roman Catholic numbers and influence. Thus, the whole insanity with its accompanying distrust, hatred and violence, had effectively been transplanted into fertile soil on the mainland.

When the coffin was carried outside, Mr Lavery was waiting with his horse and cart. I noticed that he had removed all the paraphernalia from underneath the cart. In addition, all the decoration on the sides of the cart had been covered in black cloth. He had also draped a large black cloth over the metal frame so that only the ends were open. When the coffin had been placed on the bed of the cart, all the men formed a line four-abreast behind it while all the women stood on either side of the doors of the chapel. Most of the women were crying and I saw that my mother and my grandmother were holding each other tightly as they poured out their grief. Before Mr Lavery got up on the cart, I saw him talking to my father who then came over to me.

"Willie, Ben Lavery, there, has asked if it would be alright for you to sit with him while we take your granda to the graveyard. I've told him that it's fine with me, but remember, when we get there, you will have to stay by the cart as the graveside is no place for wee ones."

I was totally surprised since it was customary that only the men went to the burial. I was also glad that I was to be given the opportunity of accompanying my grandfather on his last journey. I suppose, in a way, I felt that this meant that I was growing up and that this might be a sign that things were going to change.

The journey to the graveyard seemed to last for ages. We travelled along Clyde Street, up the Saltmarket and along Greendyke Street, past my school, and along London Street past St Alphonsus' chapel. I remember that, along the route, men doffed their caps as the procession passed them by. Many of the men and women also crossed themselves in a silent prayer. After London Street, came Great Hamilton Street and Canning Street which led to Barrowfield Toll. As the cortege made its way along London Road towards the cemetery at Dalbeth, I was amazed by all the open fields some of which had cows and sheep in them. The only other green space I had ever seen was Glasgow Green when on my way to school. Apart from the odd mansion along the way, there were no other buildings at all. Growing up as I had in crowded and filthy alleys, I was totally astounded to see so much empty space. The only other people that I saw were mostly on carts and the odd omnibus going past in both directions. I could not understand how there could be so much room here, barely two miles from Old Wynd where we had to endure such horrendous conditions.

All through the three miles distance from the chapel to the graveyard it had rained steadily. Thankfully, just after we arrived, the rain stopped. Mr Lavery spoke to a man who was standing just inside the gates and the man told him to follow him to the grave. We went about a hundred and fifty yards until we reached one end of a small pathway. As I looked along the pathway I could see a small mound of earth, which I assumed was the grave. I got down from the cart and found myself beside my grandfather, Willie. All the other men were standing around talking and smoking while they waited for Father McHugh who had left after us with the two altar boys in his pony and trap. As we waited, my grandfather took me aside and pointed to a group of large buildings.

"That's the Glasgow Water Works over there. That's where I work."

"Can I go and see them?"

"They are surely not as near as you think, Willie. See where those trees are?" he asked, pointing to a line of trees at the bottom of the hill.

When I nodded he continued: "Well, just past those trees is the river and the Water Works are at the other side in Dalmarnock."

I was so disappointed on hearing this, that I failed to appreciate the distance that my grandfather had to walk each day to and from his work. Instead, I asked if this was the same river that passed our bit. When he confirmed that it was, indeed, the river Clyde I felt some comfort in the awareness that, when I saw the river in future, I would know that those same waters had passed, not only my grandfather, but my two sisters as well.

About five minutes later, Father McHugh arrived and the coffin was carried to the grave. Four nuns had also arrived from Dalbeth Convent, which was down amongst the trees by the river. I stood by the cart as my father had told me, but I was a little upset that the two altar boys were allowed to accompany

Father McHugh to the grave while I had to stay behind, although I could hear all the prayers being said. When the prayers were finished, the nuns began to sing a hymn and I could just make out the coffin disappearing beneath the level of the ground. The priest and the altar boys came back and climbed into the trap while the nuns walked back down to the convent. Father McHugh told me he would see me at Mass on Sunday, gave the reins a snap and urged the pony to move off. As I looked back towards the graveside, I could see that all the men were still standing there and they were singing. One man would sing a verse and the others joined in at the chorus which was the only part I could hear clearly:

"So if the color we must wear be England's cruel red

Let it remind us of the blood that Irishmen have shed

And pull the shamrock from your hat, and throw it on the sod

But never fear, 'twill take root there, though underfoot 'tis trod."

This was the chorus of "The Wearin o' the Green", a song remembering events following the failed uprising by the United Irishmen in 1798. After they had finished, they all shook hands and came back towards the cart. As many as could climbed on to the bed of the cart but most would have to walk back. Before we left the graveyard, Mr Lavery lifted his seat and started to give out jars and bottles. Waxy

Mulligan, who was sitting directly behind me, told everyone that, out of respect, they should wait until they were outside the gates before partaking of the contents.

The journey back home was punctuated with singing and laughter and the odd silence when Mr Lavery spotted patrolling Peelers. Once again, I was as pleased as punch that I was with the grown-ups and even I was infected by the feeling of well-being that seemed to have superseded the sadness attached to the occasion.

Chapter Eighteen

Muck and Brass

When the funeral party returned to Back Wynd, all the men except my uncle Liam and Mr Lavery, who had to take his horse and cart back to the Saltmarket, went up to Waxy's shebeen. My uncle Liam and I went to my grandfather's house, which was crowded with women and small children, including my two cousins. The oldest cousin, William, who would have been about two years younger than me seemed to be quite shy, while his younger brother, James, appeared to be more than comfortable amongst people who were total strangers to him. When I saw him cuddling in to my grandmother, I felt a little jealous. I suppose that this would have been quite understandable given that, until that day, I had been the sole recipient of her grandmotherly affection. However, when my grandmother noticed me standing, staring at her and James, she called me over and put her left arm around me while she continued to hold James with her right.

My mother was sitting at the table chatting with my auntie Lizzie where they were joined by Uncle Liam. Soon, all three were deep in conversation.

"What's my ma going to do now my da's gone?" asked Uncle Liam.

"What do you mean, what's she going to do?" my mother replied.

"Well, she won't have his money coming in now so how is she going to pay for this place and feed herself?"

Before my mother could reply, my grandmother, who had been listening to the exchange, interrupted.

"If you don't mind, I would rather that you didn't talk about me as if I was at the other end of the street. For your information, I'll find some work at the sewing and dressmaking. I'm still young enough to do a day's work. I could have done so before but your da, the proud bugger that he was, wouldn't hear of it. So don't you be worrying about me."

"Well, ma, that's up to you but I thought that maybe you could come and live with us up in Woodside." As my uncle Liam said this, I noticed that my auntie Lizzie had a face like thunder. Obviously, this had not been a subject of prior discussion.

"Thanks, son, but I think that I'll be alright here. Mary Ann is only five minutes away and I would rather stay on here with the memories of your da."

I think that my feeling of relief that she was staying just edged out that of my auntie Lizzie. At that time, the loss of my grandmother so shortly after the loss of my grandfather, would have been devastating.

After having something to eat from the food-laden table, I asked my mother if I could go home and take Wolfe out as he had been stuck in the house since we had left earlier in the day. She told me not to be long and to come straight back.

"Can William and James come as well?" I asked my uncle Liam.

Before he could answer, my auntie Lizzie said that she didn't think that it would be a good idea in case they got lost. William seemed relieved but James started to plead with his mother that he wanted to go. He went on and on until, finally, she gave in and said that he could go.

"You mind and keep an eye on him." Uncle Liam warned me.

Just as we were leaving, I noticed that some jars had been opened and that a few people were having a drink from them. I hoped that my mother wouldn't take any as, unfortunately, on the last occasion that she had drunk alcohol, she had got very drunk, caused an argument with my father and received a beating as a consequence.

I took James' hand as we went downstairs and had to keep a firm grip as we made our way through the yards towards home as he continually tried to break free. On the way, he kept asking me all sorts of questions about everything that he saw around him. I remember thinking to myself that this is how I must seem to Goose and his father whenever I saw something new while with them. Strangely, not once did he ask about our grandfather.

When we got to my house, I opened the door and Wolfe came running out before I could stop him. He ran downstairs and round into the yard. Snatching the rope from the hook inside the door, I ran down after him, still holding James by the hand. When we reached the yard, Wolfe was just finishing his business and I took the opportunity to reach down and tie the rope round his neck. I had to let go of James' hand to accomplish the task and, when I looked round, I saw, to my horror that he had climbed up on top of the shit-pile and was doing a little dance and singing.

"I'm the king of the castle, I'm the king of the castle…"

After much cajoling and numerous threats he came back down. When I looked at his boots, I feared the worst as they were covered in muck. Not only that, but he had sunk in so far that the muck was halfway up his shins.

"You're going to get me murdered." I said, angrily.

I dragged him out of the yard and round to the bottom of the stairs, where I sat him down while I tied Wolfe to the railing.

"Right. Take off your boots and socks while I get a cloth."

I went upstairs, took a piece of rag from the cupboard, a towel which was still to be washed and the bucket which we used to take water upstairs. I went back down, filled the bucket from the tap and told James to put his now-bare feet into the water. I used the rag to clean his feet and legs and the towel to dry them. I rinsed as much of the muck out of his socks as I could and wrung them as I tight as I was able. When I looked at the boots, I was relieved to see that the insides were relatively muck-free and were easily wiped. A far greater effort was required to clean the outside, especially the lace eyelets, but eventually all traces of the muck had been removed. I used the towel to dry the boots and put them on the step where James was now sitting, being eyed curiously by Wolfe, while I emptied the bucket. To this day, I can't remember if I rinsed out the bucket before taking it back upstairs but, since no-one was sick or died over the next few days, then I must have. Either that or we were extremely lucky. As James' socks were still too wet to put on and as I only had one other pair of my own, his boots had to be put on his bare feet. I had to tie his laces as he couldn't. This took some time because I kept doing it wrong. Eventually, I had him stand up while I sat on the step behind him so that I could reach round and tie them as if I were tying my own. I put the still-damp socks in the pockets of his jacket and told him not to say anything to anybody about what had happened. I often wonder what my auntie Lizzie said when she took off his boots, saw his bare feet and then discovered his damp socks after they returned home, as the wee fellow didn't a breathe a word when we returned to my grandfather's house after taking Wolfe back upstairs.

There were not as many people there as before, but I saw that Mrs Lavery had arrived with Annie and wee Peter. Goose arrived about half an hour after James and I returned. He and I took some food from the table and went outside to sit on the stairs. When James saw us leaving, he tried to follow but his mother kept a firm hold on him. Goose told me that he had gone to the stables with his father, who was now in Waxy's. I told him what had happened with James at the shit-pile and he burst out laughing.

"Just as well you didn't have to go up after him or you would still be round there trying to clean the shit off yourselves," he chortled.

"No chance. I would just have had to wait for him. No way was I going up there. I suppose it's lucky that he didn't slip otherwise I would have been in real trouble because there's no way I would have been able to clean him up."

We sat for a while laughing as we speculated on what the reaction would have been with me turning up with James covered from head to toe in muck.

"I don't think my auntie Lizzie would have been too pleased. Imagine meeting your man's family for the first time and your wee boy ending up covered in shite." As I said this we were both convulsed with laughter. I was laughing so much that my sides hurt and tears were rolling down my cheeks. When our laughter subsided, Goose leant over and put his left arm around my shoulders and pulled me to him and said" It's good to have a wee laugh isn't, Willie."

I just nodded, in silence. As I heard the sound of lively conversation from upstairs and the loud singing emanating from the direction of Waxy's shebeen, I wondered how this could all be happening so shortly after my grandfather had been buried. I little realised that, far from being disrespectful, this was a last hurrah before the reality of his passing sank home. It would be in the days that followed that his loved-ones would begin to fully appreciate his absence. I was fortunate, in a way, that Goose was there with me. When I think of how lonely, dispirited and sad I would have felt if left to my own devices while the grown-ups were otherwise occupied, I count myself lucky that I had a pal to lean on.

Shortly afterwards, my uncle Liam and his family left for home. My grandmother and mother came downstairs with them to say goodbye. After tearful hugs and admonitions of "mind and come back down to see us", they made their way up to the alley towards the Trongate. As they passed us Goose leant over and whispered in my ear.

"Can you smell shite, Willie?"

"Ssh. Somebody will hear you" I whispered back giving his side a slight nudge with my elbow and trying my best not to laugh. Fortunately nobody *had* heard him and my mother and grandmother went back upstairs leaving us on our own. We decided to move up a bit closer to Waxy's so that we could hear the singing. When we reached the close, the man with the scar and the lantern, which was as yet unlit, was there. He recognised me and it was evident that he knew Goose already.

"Right, young Lavery what are you and young Toner up to?"

"Nothing, Mr Kinsella and his name's McCart not Toner. We just want to listen to the singing if that's all right."

"Well, there's more than a few good voices in today so you'll not be disappointed. You can go through and stand at the bottom of the stairs, but if anyone comes out then you'll need to shift your arses back out here right away."

As he said this, he stepped aside and we walked through. We sat at the bottom of the stairs and

141

listened to the singing, which we could now hear much more clearly. As I remember, it was a mixture of popular songs, such as we heard at the Britannia and traditional Irish songs, a few of them sung in Irish, with which I was only slightly familiar through hearing them from my grandfathers on occasion. Suddenly, the singing stopped and I nearly jumped out of my skin when I heard a very loud and unfamiliar sound, which quickly mellowed into a tune I had never heard before. Goose gave a start too and asked the guard where the sound came from.

"Sure, that will be Barney Donovan and his cornet playing The Wind That Shakes The Barley," he replied before starting to hum in time with the music. At one point the guard stopped humming and began to sing.

"Twas hard the woeful words to frame

To break the ties that bound us

But harder still to bear the shame

Of foreign chains around us

And so I said, 'The mountain glen

I'll seek at morning early

And join the bold United Men

While soft winds shake the barley.'"

The music continued for some minutes more and I could hear the sound of applause when the tune was ended. The guard remarked that Barney Donovan sure blew a fine tune and it was just a pity that he had learned to play when he was a boy soldier in the English army.

As darkness began to fall, Mr Kinsella, whose lantern was now lit, called for us to go back home. We went back to my grandfather's house, where only my grandmother, mother, Mrs Lavery and the children remained.

"Where have you been?" the two mothers asked, almost in unison.

"We've just been up the Wynd." Goose answered with a half-truth.

Satisfied with the answer, his mother said her goodbyes and they all left to go home with Goose making exaggerated sniffing motions as he passed me. Again, I only just managed to avoid laughing. Shortly afterwards, my mother put her coat on to leave.

"I better get Willie home, mammy, before it gets too dark. Will you be alright here on your own?"

"I'll be fine, Mary Ann. Just you get the wee fellow home safe and sound. I'll just sit for a wee while and have a wee chat to your da before I go to bed. If you have time, could you maybe come round and see me after you take Willie to school tomorrow?"

"Of course, mammy. Do you need me to bring anything round for you?"

"Not at all. Look at all this stuff still here." She replied pointing to the table which still held a considerable amount of food. "In fact, you should take some of that with you for your breakfast tomorrow and for James to take for his work. Willie, I've spoken to your ma and she thinks it will be alright for you to keep Wolfe for good. I think it's better that he has somebody younger to look after him and I know he likes you too. "

"Th-thanks very much, granny," I stuttered in reply, as my mother did as my grandmother had suggested, wrapping food in some of the paper that was lying around. My grandmother hugged us both before we left, as my mother promised, once again, that she would visit the next day. As we walked home, I eventually plucked up the courage to ask my mother to explain something that had been bothering me for a few minutes.

"Mammy, what did my granny mean when she said that she was going to have a wee chat with your da?"

"Well, that's exactly what she's going to do, son. As far as she's concerned, your granda is still in the house and always will be. You'll be the same anytime you go back. You'll always remember your granda and when you always remember someone, then they will always be there. It's just the same as when you pray to Jesus and to God. You can't see them, but you know they are there, just the same."

It may seem strange to many but this simplistic explanation was probably the most comforting statement I had heard since my grandfather's death. True or not, her explanation instilled in me a sense of continuity, replacing the feeling of despair at my loss and I held her hand just that little bit tighter as we made our way through the deepening darkness.

Chapter Nineteen

Trains and Brains

The winter of that year was like any other, but the following spring was unlike any I had experienced before. It was not that the weather was unusual, but rather the momentous changes taking place around us. Major demolition of a large area north of Jackson Street, including that of the Theatre Royal, cleared the final obstacle to the construction of the new railway. The pillars that had been built in the river were now topped by a massive cast-iron bridge. Hundreds of men were now working on the construction of massive brick-built viaducts which would support the railway. In addition, bridges were also being built across Bridgegate, the Saltmarket and Stockwell Street. New tramways were also being installed in Stockwell Street and Trongate. The new Fish Market had been completed over the winter, but this proved to be more of an inconvenience to my mother because of the roundabout route she had to take to reach it due to the closure of the Wynds. Mr Lavery was not best-pleased with any of the work that was going on because of the extensive disruption that was, understandably, taking place due to all the massive works. It now took us the best part of an hour to negotiate our way to the docks on Saturday mornings and sometimes longer when we returned in the afternoons.

However, one of the major beneficiaries of the ongoing construction works was my grandmother. She had tried to find a job sewing or dressmaking, but had been unsuccessful and had, therefore, to rely on a meagre income for doing small pieces of work for local people. I had tried to give her some of the money I had saved, but she wouldn't hear of it, but she promised to keep my secret when I explained how I had been working with Mr Lavery. Fortunately for her, a more lucrative opportunity soon became available.

As the construction works progressed, a new street stretching from Stockwell Street to King Street and named Osborne Street, was laid out. This meant that the remaining parts of the Wynds now had exits at the bottom ends. From this street it was possible to see all the works taking place to the east, west and south of where we lived. My grandmother's house was only about ten yards from the street and she began to sell food, mainly soup, to many of the construction workers. The idea had come from Waxy Mulligan. Many of the workers tended to frequent Waxy's shebeen at the end of their shifts and were always looking for something to eat owing to the fact that most of them were itinerant workers who lived in the camp on the site. Waxy had suggested to my grandmother that, since they had to pass her house to reach his place, then she might be able to earn a few shillings by feeding them before he got the rest of their money. My grandmother agreed and, within a very short period of time, she had a substantial number of regular customers. In addition, many of her customers also bought food from her at their midday break. Such was the level of business that, on one occasion, her house was raided

146

by the Peelers who assumed that the numbers of men frequenting the house indicated that it was being used as a haven for prostitution. When they realised their mistake they actually apologised and asked if they could have something to eat. Although it must have been enormously difficult for her to be civil with them, considering what had happened to my grandfather, she judged, correctly, that it would do her no harm to stay on their better side, so feed them she did. They were most appreciative, but not so appreciative that they felt that they should pay for the food.

My grandmother's most popular dish was sheep's-head soup. The first time I watched her making it was an education in how the ingenuity of the poor was such that even the unthinkable became edible. She put the sheep's head in a basin and covered it with methylated spirits. She then lit a taper from the fire and set the head alight. The spirits quickly burned off most of the hair from the head so that only a fine stubble remained. She then put the head on the table, cut out the eyes and the tongue and split the skull with a large cleaver. She scraped the brains out through the split and put them in a dish with the eyes and tongue. The head was then put into a pot of cold water and brought to the boil. This water was then thrown away and the head was then put in the pot along with chopped-up carrots, turnip, onion and potatoes, seasoned, covered with water and left to boil for five hours after which the soup was thickened with flour.

The tongue, brains and eyes were boiled in another pot, then they were chopped up and mixed with breadcrumbs and minced parsley and seasoned with

147

salt and pepper. An egg was used to bind the mixture before it was formed into small balls, rolled in flour and baked in the oven. . When ready, they were sold at a farthing each to accompany the soup, which she sold for a penny-halfpenny. By only having to pay three pence for each sheep's head, my grandmother was able to exist on the income she made from this enterprise. She didn't make as much money on Fridays since most of the workers were Catholics and she had to provide them with fish, which was more expensive for her to buy.

A major highlight in my life at that time was my school proficiency test in the early summer. The test consisted of being able to recite the alphabet and the times-tables. In addition I had to demonstrate an acceptable level of reading, writing and arithmetic skills before I would be allowed to leave. I was fortunate that I had been a good learner and had had little difficulty with my schoolwork. Consequently, I achieved the required proficiency and was now free from school forever, or so I thought. My freedom would last for less than nine weeks. New education legislation had been enacted that had required the Church to acquire premises in Ropework Lane beside the chapel and to establish a new school. Although I was almost eleven years old and not subject to the terms of this legislation, the Church authorities were insistent that all Catholic children should attend school until the summer of their eleventh year. As a victim of this policy, I was less than pleased but my displeasure was as nothing compared to that of the parents of the children now caught up in this education trap. Where a ten or eleven year old would normally be contributing to the family income, he or she would now be stuck in school for, at least, an additional year. However, there was no choice to be had. The Church had spoken and that was that. Although, at the time, this new departure was less than welcome to the Catholic population, I have to admit that this additional time spent at school may well have made all the difference to the future prospects of many of the recipients of this unwelcomed opportunity.

My nine weeks of freedom offered me the opportunity of a different education altogether. Mrs Lavery had asked my mother if I could spend some time with her and the family when they went hawking. My father, who had become aware of my friendship with the Laverys, gave a grudging approval when my mother raised the subject with him. I could tell that he was not completely happy about this and I didn't understand why he hadn't lost his temper as he usually did when he wasn't pleased about something or other. What I didn't know then was the level of influence that Mr Lavery and the Ribbon Society in general, exerted within the various Irish communities in the city.

Consequently, most of my weekdays were then spent travelling around the more prosperous districts of Glasgow knocking on doors and acquiring clothing and other items, which the Laverys would later sell on. At first, I accompanied Mrs Lavery, while Goose and Annie accompanied their father. I learned to arrange a basket which would be carried around and from which items would be offered to householders in return for what they gave to us. Each basket contained five fairly large coloured-glass dishes, usually red, which were arranged in a circle around the inside. Within this circle, smaller,

149

cheaper items like crockery and plaster ornaments, were arranged in a bed of straw and covered with a cloth.

"Now remember, Willie, this is called the flash", Mrs Lavery said pointing at the glass plates. "We don't normally give these to anyone at all. Always offer something from underneath the cover. If they won't accept your offer then just walk away. Most of the time they will call you back and take whatever you're offering as they have already decided to get rid of their stuff anyway."

As time went on, I learned the truth of her teaching. I carried the basket for her as we went round the doors. Although wee Peter could now just about walk, she continued to carry him wrapped in a shawl in such a fashion as to leave her hands free. Things turned out just as she had predicted although, on numerous occasions, the closing of a door would be accompanied with comments about robbing, cheating Gypsy bastards. When I asked Mrs Lavery what a Gypsy was, she laughed as she told me that everybody assumed that all hawkers were Gypsies, who were, in fact, different tribes of Romany travelling people who could be found in many different countries. She also told me that she did come from a Kale Gypsy family in Wales, but they had disowned her when she met and married her husband, as the Gypsy tradition more or less forbade marriage to anyone from outside the Gypsy community. We spent whole days doing this, stopping only for something to eat and drink or finding a reasonably private place to satisfy our toilet needs. Mr Lavery, or even Goose, sometimes, would move the cart along the street for maybe fifty yards and we others would be busy moving back and forth loading the cart with our booty.

On other days, we would take the booty to sell in the Bazaar. Market Lane had been closed due to the construction works that were taking place. When construction was completed, the lane was reopened and became known as the Irish Market. I thoroughly enjoyed the selling days in the Bazaar. While we children mostly just sat around, Mr and Mrs Lavery were busy calling out to all and sundry about the excellent quality and reasonable prices of their goods. What I liked most were the negotiations that took place between the Laverys and their potential customers. Most exchanges were good-natured and humorous and would usually be concluded at a mutually-satisfactory price and accompanied by a handshake and some mild name-calling.

For my labours, I was paid the princely sum of three pence a day. On the first day, when I told Mr Lavery that I didn't want any money, he became quite stern and insisted that I take it.

"This is money that you've earned Willie McCart. It's your money not mine. We work as a family, we eat as a family and, when times are hard, we suffer as a family. Soon enough, you may have to find work with someone who's only interest will be in squeezing as much toil as he can from you at the minimum of cost and, when you're of no further use, will think nothing of casting you aside like a piece of rubbish.

I was slightly taken aback at the vehemence accompanying his words and I meekly accepted the money. When I got home, I always gave the money

151

to my mother except for my Saturday money which I still added to the pouch under the floor. My mother was delighted with the money, which she never, ever told my father about, and I, for my part, felt proud that I was making a contribution, although I was more pleased that I was bringing her a little happiness. Unfortunately, any happiness she felt would soon be brought to an abrupt end.

Chapter Twenty

Blood and Iron

My second "final" year at school was just like any other notwithstanding the fact that I was now attending the new St Andrew's school in Ropework Lane. My previous school, also St Andrew's, was now known as St Alphonsus'. To my horror, I found that my new school was also staffed by nuns. My new teacher was Sister Mary Theresa who was much younger than all the nuns teaching in my old school and, much to my surprise, was altogether more pleasant than her sisters. She still had to maintain discipline, of course, but when she punished the children, she displayed a humanity which, until then, I would not have associated with the "brides of Christ". It seemed to me that it pained her to have to dole out the punishments she did, but I have no doubt that a failure to maintain discipline on her part would have had serious consequences for her. I also have no doubt that a lack of discipline could well have led to chaos in the classroom, given that, like myself, most of my classmates did not want to be there in the first place.

I had spent most of the previous four weeks helping my mother and grandmother in the kitchen, as the Laverys had gone on their summer travels. I had become quite adept at preparing the food that she cooked and sold on. The number of customers had risen so much that she now needed two if not three sheep's heads every day as well as an increased amount of bread, flour, vegetables and other foodstuffs. Fortunately, Mr Lavery had made arrangements with his brother, Peter, who was now working in the slaughterhouse in the Gallowgate, to supply the heads and other meat at a reduced rate. This necessitated an early morning trip for my mother and me to collect these items, so that my grandmother would have enough time to cook them. We would leave at the same time as my father, but although we had to pass the Saracen Iron Works on Dovehill on our journey, he insisted that we had to split up as he always met up with some fellow-workers and he didn't want us with him. I didn't understand why this should be but I knew better than to raise any objection. I used to wonder if he was ashamed of us for some reason, but I would rather believe that, given the earthy nature of some male conversation, his reluctance was mainly to avoid discomfiting his mates, whose conversation subjects would have been necessarily limited by the presence of a woman and child.

When we arrived at the slaughterhouse and market, we had to go all the way in to the buildings, as Peter couldn't leave his workplace. At first I found the sight of the animals being killed, gutted, skinned and butchered to be horrifying and sickening, but my horror was quickly replaced by a fascination and a total lack of squeamishness at the surrounding carnage. I was also full of admiration at the skills of the skinners as I watched them with their long-bladed knives expertly removing the skins from the dead animals, which were hanging on rows of meat-hooks. My mother, however, never got used

154

to the sights and she would wait outside while I went in and bought that day's supply. After only a short time of my doing this, I became quite well-known to many of the men working there and I became the butt of their good-natured humour.

"Look, the little piggy's come to market." "Not much meat on him." "Not enough for a pot of soup." "Does your mammy know you're out?"

These were amongst the most repeated remarks I heard as I made my way into the bowels of the building. All of these remarks were accompanied by laughter on all sides. How incongruous it would have seemed to a visitor to hear such laughter in the midst of all the slaughter, butchery and streams of blood flowing down the channels for collection. If this could be viewed by some as a vision of hell it would not compare with the real hellish experience that I and my family were shortly to undergo.

I remember I was sitting on the floor playing with Wolfe after coming home from school while my mother was sitting knitting. As I was "a big boy now" and the new school was closer than the old one, I didn't need my mother to take me to school or to fetch me home any longer. We were startled by a loud knock at the door and Wolfe had jumped up and started barking as loudly as was possible for a dog of his small stature.

My mother shushed Wolfe out of the way as she rose to answer the knocking. When she opened the door, I heard a strange voice.

"Mrs McCart? I'm Michael Cole and I work with your man. I'm sorry to tell you that James has had an accident and has been taken to the Royal Infirmary for treatment. I think that you should maybe go up there right away as it looks quite bad and they might have to send for the priest."

I could see that my mother was visibly shocked but, surprisingly, she didn't lose her composure in the way that she had when she thought I was going to be put out of school. Instead, she thanked the man and took her coat and my jacket off the hook at the back of the door.

"Willie, you go round to your granny's and stay there till I come back."

"But mammy..."

"No buts, just do as you're told" she interrupted, her voice angry and close to breaking.

I didn't argue any further and I put my jacket and cap on to leave. As Wolfe was still barking loudly my mother told me to take him with me in case he didn't settle down, as this would only upset the neighbours. We all came downstairs together, but my mother went up towards the Trongate while I made my way through the yards to Back Wynd. When I arrived at my grandmother's house, I repeated the message that my mother had been given by Michael Cole.

"Oh my God" she exclaimed as she sat down and lifted the apron she was wearing up to her mouth. "Oh sweet Jesus, Mary and Joseph, please let him be all right" she said, tears welling up in her eyes.

When I saw her tears, the realisation dawned that, despite my mother's almost calm demeanour, this was a serious situation. If I had been older, Mr

Cole's mention of a priest would have brought this awareness home at once.

"You'd better keep your jacket on, Willie for we'll have to go down to Bridgegate and tell your auntie Hannah to let your granda know when he comes home from work. But you should leave Wolfe here till we come back."

We had to go the long way round down the Saltmarket because of all the construction works, but when we reached my grandfather's house, there was no-one at home. My grandmother knocked on a neighbour's door and a woman who answered agreed to pass on the message about my father when someone came home.

As we were walking back up the Saltmarket I realised that tears were now running down my cheeks. My grandmother noticed my tears, stopped walking and bent over to comfort me.

"Don't worry, son. I'm sure your da's going to be all right."

I felt no comfort whatsoever in her words, as I still had a clear memory of a similar attempt at comforting by Mrs Lavery when I was worried about my grandfather.

"Can we not go and see if he's all right?"

"Oh the Royal Infirmary's awful far away, Willie."

I knew exactly how far away the Royal Infirmary was, as I had passed it many times with the Laverys, especially when we visited Goose's auntie Alice.

"But I want to see my da" I insisted as my crying became uncontrollable.

"I want to see my da. I don't want my da to die. I didn't mean all those things I said. I don't really hate him. I want to see my da."

By now, I was sitting on the ground and my grandmother was hunched down trying to cuddle me. I pushed her away quite forcibly which must have been a shock to her. My reaction must also have been the catalyst for her to change her mind.

"All right then but I'm telling you now. When we get there you'd better behave yourself. Don't you be upsetting your ma, as she's got enough on her plate as it is."

These were the first and only angry words that my grandmother ever said to me. In a way, I suppose that her admonition was probably aimed as much at herself as it was at me.

As my grandmother had said, the Royal Infirmary was quite far away. We had to walk up the Saltmarket to Glasgow Cross and on into High Street. As we made our way up the long hill we did so in total silence. Never having been in an Iron Works, I had no idea what type of accident might have befallen my father and I didn't think my grandmother would know either. When we neared the top of High Street, where the College used to be before the new one was built at Gilmorehill, I could see a good number of men busily involved in some type of building work. This was, in fact the construction site for a railway station on the new line being established between Glasgow and Monklands. We crossed over Duke Street and continued up High

Street, the hill now becoming steeper, so much so that my grandmother insisted on stopping for five minutes as she needed to rest. When we finally reached the junction of Kirk Street and Drygate, opposite the Townhead Gas Works, the full frontage of the Royal Infirmary came into view. To our right was the cathedral of St Mungo and I could see a large graveyard dominated by a statue of John Knox on a high pillar, which seemed to be immediately behind the cathedral. This graveyard, the Necropolis, was, in fact, situated on the far bank of the Molendinar Burn and was accessed via the Bridge of Sighs. Seeing the graves, I was, once again, filled with dread and I tried to quicken my steps to reach the hospital entrance, which was directly in front of us, but my grandmother had a tight grip on my hand and I was slowed to her pace. We went up the stairs and into a large open hall where we were stopped by a man wearing a strange jacket with beading and brass buttons. He looked at us with some distaste and demanded to know why we were there. When my grandmother told him that we were looking for a Mr James McCart who had been brought to the hospital for emergency treatment, he informed us that we would have to go outside, turn right and enter through a small gateway. Evidently, it would have been unthinkable that the likes of us should be allowed to use the internal route. Unfortunately, we did as we were told and we entered through the designated access. I say "unfortunately" because we had no sooner entered than we heard screams of pain, screams that I recognised, somehow, as being my father's. Once again, I was consumed by fear and I would have burst into tears if I hadn't caught sight of my mother who was seated in the far corner of

159

what was a small crowded room. Remembering my grandmother's admonition, I made a superhuman effort not to cry. She, however, was sobbing into the apron, which she was still wearing under her coat, having forgotten to remove it in her rush to leave the house. She made to rise so that my grandmother could sit down, as there were no other spaces available on the long benches that lined the walls, but my grandmother insisted that she remained seated. As I moved closer to her she dropped her apron and held me so close that I could feel every tremor in her body as she told my grandmother the details of what had occurred, as had been related to her by Mr Cole, who had accompanied her as far as Blackfriars Street before he had gone back to his work.

My father was an iron puddler. Iron puddling was a process which involved the opening of the furnace so that the molten iron could be stirred. Normally, the gases generated by the smelting process would be extracted through the flue of the furnace. For some reason, the flue had become blocked and, when my father opened the door of the furnace, the build-up of gases had exploded through the door and he had been engulfed by their searing heat. His whole front had been charred such that all his clothes had burnt through and the remnants had stuck to his seared flesh. His face had been very badly burned and the remains of his cap and hair were almost fused to his head. Those injuries may well have been survivable but his inhalation of hot gases including phosphorous, sulphur and manganese meant that his lungs were damaged beyond repair. However, at that time, all we knew was that he had been accidentally burned. The screaming continued unabated for some time, but, gradually, the volume decreased until all we could hear was a continuous moan. A door opened and a priest came out and asked for the family of James McCart. When my mother and grandmother approached him, he told them that my father was unconscious at the moment and that the doctor had tried to relieve his pain as much as possible. He also told them that he had given my father the Last Sacraments as the doctor held out little hope for my father's recovery. My mother burst into tears once again, as did my grandmother. I, however, was frozen in horror. I remember feeling that, somehow, this was all my fault. At those times when he had been beating my mother, I had wished that he was dead and now this was going to happen. My feelings of guilt were so strong that I started to walk away from my mother towards the door to the street, my whole body shaking and tears streaming down my face. My grandmother caught me by the shoulders and turned me around to face her.

"Where are you going, Willie? You have to stay here with me and your ma."

"But granny it's all my fault. I've wished that he was dead a lot of times. But I didn't really mean it, granny. I didn't really mean it."

"Listen, son. I heard you say that earlier on as well but you're wrong. People don't die just because other people wish for it. Everybody says things that they don't really mean. Sometimes I used to tell your granda that *I* hated *him* but he and I knew that it wasn't true. It's just something that we say when we're upset. And remember, only God decides when people die, not wee boys. Now let's get back over to your ma and don't let's be hearing any more about it."

As we crossed the room towards my mother, a woman came through the door that the priest had used and asked for Mrs McCart. When my mother identified herself, the woman repeated what the priest had said regarding my father's condition. What she said next, however, will stay with me until my dying day.

"You realise, Mrs McCart, that we have given your husband all the emergency treatment that we are required to do. Should he survive the coming night you will have to make arrangements to have him removed either to your home, which I would not recommend, or across to the City Poorhouse in Parliamentary Road, where hospital care facilities might be available."

The blandness of her statement and the apparent air of aloofness in which it was delivered, took me aback completely.

"Why can't my da stay here? This is a massive place with hundreds of windows. I saw them outside. What use is a hospital if it doesn't take care of sick people?" I thought to myself.

Even at my relatively young age I perceived that this was an inhuman way to treat people who were suffering such distress. However, what was more shocking was the fact that my mother and grandmother made absolutely no objection and nodded their assent.

As it turned out, my mother didn't have any choice to make because at twenty past five that day, my father died.

Chapter Twenty One

Moonlight and Moses

My father's funeral was totally different from that of my grandfather the previous year. His body had been brought home in a closed coffin because of the extent of the injuries he had suffered. My mother's penny policy barely covered the cost of the coffin and its transportation to our house and the cemetery fees. I found out much later that Father McHugh had insisted that there be no donation made to the chapel. My grandfather and my uncle Willie helped my mother with some money for the wake but if it hadn't been for Mr Lavery who, once again, made his horse and cart available, my mother would have found it well nigh impossible to avoid my father being buried in a pauper's grave. The other major differences were that less people attended and there were no green rosettes to be seen. Additionally, I was allowed to stand by the graveside as my father's coffin was lowered into the ground. There had been no memorable eulogy delivered at the Mass and there was no singing at the graveside, apart from the hymn sung by the nuns from the convent. Similarly, the journey home was almost as silent as the cortege had been on the way out. Although my father was evidently not as popular as my grandfather had been, it saddened me to think of how so few people felt it necessary to pay their respects, even if they did not like him very much.

Two days after the funeral, my mother informed me that we would be leaving our house in Old Wynd and moving in with my grandmother. This was necessary since my mother had no work skills to speak of as she had married my father when she was seventeen and had never done any work outside of the house. My grandmother had taught her how to sew when she was young, but she was never very good at it. It was decided that we would leave on the Thursday night so as to avoid paying the landlord's factor who would be coming to collect the rent on the Friday night. This was what was known as a moonlight flit, a not unknown occurrence even in this day and age. My uncle Willie duly arrived with a handcart on the Thursday and, after only two trips, the sum total of our possessions was transferred to my grandmother's house. I had a major difficulty in removing my hidden hoard from beneath the floor without being seen by my mother. I had asked my grandmother if I should now tell my mother about the money but she advised me to keep it secret for the time being.

"Your ma won't need it just now, Willie, as we'll all be living here together, but there may come a time when she will. So just you keep a hold of it for now."

I didn't object but I asked her if she would look after it for me. She agreed that she would and that she would hide it at the bottom of her sewing box that she kept beneath the bed.

It must have seemed a little strange to my mother that she should be back living there so long after she had left to start out on her married life. I, myself, got used to living there fairly quickly and I imagine that, to Wolfe, it was just a simple homecoming. The only drawback for me was that it was a little bit further from school and meant that the freezing cold journeys were that little bit longer. One thing I never really got used to was my grandmother's presence in our shared bed rather than that of my father. It would be a long time before I woke in the early morning and failed to be surprised by his absence.

The days, weeks and months began to follow an increasingly familiar pattern. On weekdays there would be school and Saturdays would be spent with the Laverys. When my mother wasn't around, I would give my money to my grandmother and she would put it away for me. My grandmother and my mother, who was now helping her all the time, continued to make a living selling food.

In the early summer, my days at St Andrew's school finally came to an end. Surprisingly, I was not as overjoyed as I had been when I thought I had finished at my previous school. I liked Sister Mary Theresa and I found that I had actually learned quite a lot and that I had enjoyed the learning process in itself. However, any regrets I had about leaving school were far outweighed by thoughts about the world that would be opening before me. My uncle Willie had told my mother that he could get me a job in the mill, for which I would be paid sixpence a day for working from seven in the morning to five at night, six days a week. These jobs were quite common for boys and girls of my age as we were small enough to crawl under the machines to clear snags or clean the floors underneath. Being so young, I had no idea how horrendous the working conditions would be and I urged my mother to accept his offer. Fortunately for me, a better offer was made by Mr Lavery. He told my mother that he was willing to give me a job with him and that he would pay me nine pence a day for five days. He knew that I did not tell my mother about my Saturday money, so he told her that I didn't need to work on a Saturday, but that I could still go with them if I wanted.

Thus it was that I now became a fully-fledged hawker. I very quickly became quite adept in my dealings, but nowhere near as successful as Goose. I was now about an inch taller than he was and his smaller stature, his fresh complexion and his curly fair hair seemed to appeal to most of the householders more than my freckled face topped by a mop of curly red hair and an old flat cap. Nevertheless, I did my bit and earned my nine pence a day. On particularly good days my money was increased but, even when things didn't go to well, I never got any less than my nine pence. An additional benefit was that I could have my pick of the clothing we collected, but only after negotiating a price with Mr Lavery. I enjoyed haggling with him but I think that he let me win because, generally, the amount agreed was always nearer my original offer than to his original asking price.

The days spent hawking were not entirely taken up by serious business. The days would also be punctuated by laughter when we would swap stories about some of the different customers we had dealt with and about all of their different foibles, some of which were quite unbelievable, such as the time that Mr Lavery had knocked on a door and the woman who answered had been so drunk that she had started to take her clothes off because she didn't have anything else to exchange but she "really fancied one of those nice, red dishes". When Mr Lavery told the story he quipped that she was so ugly that he offered her a dish if she would put her clothes back on. I, too, encountered a really strange householder, but, as it turned out, all was not what it seemed.

We were working in Buckingham Terrace, which is lined on one side by large, fancy houses. We were about halfway along when Mr Lavery told me to go to a house at a window of which I could see a man's face. I climbed the steps to the door and gave three raps on the brass knocker, which was in the shape of a lion's head. After two or three minutes, the door was opened by an old man wearing a woman's dress. He had a patch over his left eye and a long grey beard. When he demanded to know what I wanted, he did so in a high-pitched voice as if he were pretending to be a woman.

"Mr er Mrs er I w-was w-wondering i-if..."

"Speak up, boy. I don't have all day." He interrupted in the same high-pitch.

"D-do y-you h-have..."

"Do I have what? Are you mental? Can't you speak right? Have you never seen a woman before?"

I didn't answer immediately, as I debated with myself whether I should beat a hasty retreat. However, I held my nerve and managed to blurt out my usual spiel, upon which he told me to wait as he went back inside to look. When he came back he was dressed normally and the patch was now over his right eye.

"What do you want," he asked in a normal male voice.

"But I just told you," I replied somewhat indignantly.

"I've never clapped eyes on you before you cheeky little bastard. Oh, hang on a minute. You must mean my sister. She's my twin, you know, but most people don't believe that because we're nothing like each other."

Totally confused and just a little bit ticked off, I had decided to give up what was, obviously, a lost cause, when I heard the sound of loud laughter from the street behind me. When I turned around, all the Laverys were standing there laughing like crazy and, I swear that even wee Peter was having a hearty chortle.

"Willie," said Mr Lavery. "Let me introduce you to my uncle Moses."

When I turned back to the door, the man was also laughing. Unbeknownst to me, Mr Lavery had signalled to his uncle as my back was turned and I had been well and truly set up.

"He did the same thing to me, Willie," said Goose. "But I didn't handle it as well as you."

Goose had, in fact, told Uncle Moses to fuck off and had been rewarded by a clout from his father.

We all went in to Uncle Moses' house, where we spent the next hour chatting while having something to eat and drink. Mr Lavery told his uncle about me and about my father and grandfather.

"Sure, that's a crying shame, youngster," Uncle Moses said, sympathetically.

"Th-thank you, s-sir," I replied, unsure of how to address him.

"Just you be calling me Uncle Moses, same as everybody else. Sure aren't you just like one of the family now. Isn't that right Ben?"

When Mr Lavery nodded in agreement, Goose gave a broad smile and clapped me on the back. In spite of my best efforts, my eyes were filled with tears. I was so overcome by a feeling of such gratitude at the kindness that these people had always shown me now culminating in their regarding me as part of the family. Somehow, this appeared to make up, in some way, for my recent losses. When Mr Lavery saw my tears he tousled my hair and joked.

"Oh come on, Willie. It's not that bad although I wouldn't want Goose for a brother either."

The humour in his remark proved sufficient to stop my tears and to cause my features to break into a broad grin and the general conversation resumed. Before we left, Uncle Moses gave all the children a little gift. He gave me a small brass spyglass and advised me to use it regularly so that I would "see things coming". This remark caused more laughter and even I appreciated the wit behind his advice, given how I had been set up.

On the way back home, I learned that Uncle Moses had gone to sea when he was a boy but had returned, apparently quite wealthy, after twenty three years. The family believed that he had acquired this wealth through his involvement in piracy in the China Sea, but he always maintained that he had married a wealthy English widow in India but she had died and he had inherited her money. When I remarked that I had never met anyone called Moses before, Mr Lavery laughed as he replied.

"That's all down to my grandfather who was a great man for the bible. He decided that he would name all his children after the prophets and other people in it. So we have Isaac, my own father, Uncle Moses, Uncle Jeremiah and Uncle Elias. My auntie Ezekiel has never been happy with her name, but she never had any choice in the matter," he explained dissolving into a fit of laughter. As we all laughed with him, Mrs Lavery interrupted.

"What about your own father. He called all his children after popes. There's Benedict, Peter, Leo and Pius..."

"Aye, maybe so, but at least my sister's name is Margaret and not Gregory the Great," he retorted and we all started laughing again.

This set the tone for the rest of the journey home and my head was filled with an imagined likeness of Mr Lavery's Auntie Ezekiel, wondering if she, too, had a long beard like Uncle Moses.

Chapter Twenty Two

Wanderers' Lust

When it came time for the Laverys to leave on their summer trip, I was delighted when my mother agreed that I could go with them. On the morning of our departure, she took me round to their house in the Saltmarket. When we reached the close, Mr Lavery and Goose were just coming out carrying some boxes, which they put on the cart. The horse, Sandy, was busily munching on the oats and hay inside the nosebag, which was hanging from his head. I had learned that, when the nosebag was on, the horse tended to stand still without having to be tethered.

"The top of the morning to you, Mrs McCart, Willie," said Mr Lavery heartily.

"Good morning to you, Mr Lavery and please call me Mary Ann."

"Mary Ann it is then. And it's Ben to you. Now what's this you have here?" he asked pointing to a bundle she was carrying.

"Oh it's just some clothes and some food for Willie."

"Nonsense. Sure he'll have all the food he needs along with us and any clothes he needs we can pick up as we go."

Because of the limited space on the cart they always carried as little as possible so as to make more room for the goods they acquired. This was even more vital when they faced a much longer journey with the corresponding demands on the horse. At their insistence, we followed Goose and his father upstairs to their house. Mrs Lavery warmly welcomed us and invited my mother to sit down and have a cup of tea. While the two mothers had their tea I helped Mr Lavery, Goose and Annie to carry other things downstairs to the cart, while wee Peter sat in a corner having a semblance of conversation with some rag dolls. Goose also took the opportunity to show me around his house. Unlike us, they had two rooms one of which was half filled with clothes. There was also a bed, a cot and one or two other items of furniture.

"This is where me, Annie and Peter sleep," Goose informed me.

"You mean that you and Annie have that big bed there all to yourselves?" I replied with a twinge of envy.

"Aye. But only till Peter's a bit older, then it will be the three of us."

As I looked at the pile of clothes in the room, I wondered where everything else was, because we had certainly gathered much more than this and we hadn't been selling for at least a week. When I asked Goose he crooked his finger and motioned me out to the landing.

"See that door there?" He asked pointing across the landing. "That's our house too but it only has one room and we store most of our stuff in that. My da says that, when I get married, I can live in there, but God knows where he'll store his stuff then."

I found the whole idea of Goose being married to be extremely amusing, not least because, apart from Annie, I had never seen him as much as talk to a girl, unless it was a girl who answered a door while we were out hawking.

Finally, the cart was loaded and we were ready to leave. Before I climbed on to the cart, my mother kissed me, warned me to behave and to do as I was told. As the cart moved off up the Saltmarket, she stood at the close, the bundle at her feet, waving with one hand while wiping the tears from her eyes with the other. I felt a brief twinge of regret that I was leaving her behind, but, by the time Mr Lavery steered Sandy round into the Gallowgate, all thoughts of my mother disappeared, as I imagined the adventures that lay ahead.

By the end of the first day, we had reached as far as Baillieston in the Parish of Cadder. Mr Lavery was well-acquainted with a Mr Wilson, who owned a farm and who allowed us to sleep in his barn, on condition that we helped him with the milking the following morning. After Mr Lavery had unhitched the horse, he brought it into the barn and put it in a stall beside the farmer's two huge horses. We had a meal of dried meat, cheese and bread accompanied by hot tea, which Mrs Lavery had brewed over a small fire outside in the farmyard Then, as the sun set, we all lay down on the hay where we were kept warm by the blankets that had been brought from underneath the cart. Despite the unfamiliar surroundings, I fell asleep almost immediately and only awoke when nudged by Goose early next morning. While Mrs Lavery and Annie took care of Peter and prepared our breakfast, I helped Goose to herd the cattle towards the shed where Mr Lavery and the farmer were doing the milking. As this was the first time I had ever been close to any large animal, excepting horses, I was more than a little intimidated, but by following Goose's lead and the judicious wielding of a large stick, I found the cattle relatively easy to control.

"It's just a matter of showing them who's in charge," advised Goose as me made to give a smart swipe of his stick to the nearest cow. Unfortunately, he slipped and the blow missed the cow's rear and caught its udder instead. The cow gave an angry bellow and kicked out. Goose was caught directly on the chest and was sent flying backwards. I ran over to make sure that he hadn't been injured, but found that he had had a soft landing in a large heap of soiled straw and horse manure. As he was struggling to get up, cursing and threatening retribution to the offending cow, I could not resist the temptation to have a wee dig.

"Can you smell shite, Willie" I quoted mimicking the exaggerated sniffing motions he had made at my grandmother's house.

"I'll fucking smell shite *you*," he retorted as he started to chase me across the farmyard waving his stick.

"Hoi, you two. That's enough arsing about. We've got work to do or we'll never get going. Now get those cows in here and be quick about it."

At the sound of Mr Lavery's voice, we very quickly returned to our task. I continued to make the sniffing motions, but Goose laughed along with me. His laughter didn't last long, however, when his mother saw the state of his clothes, which she had to wash before we left. In spite of his protests, she insisted on washing the muck from Goose with water from a trough. Although it was summer, this water was still very cold and I whispered "goose bumps" to Annie who had a fit of the giggles. Goose glared at her and eyed me with suspicion as to my part in setting Annie off.

Over the course of the next few days, we travelled on through Coatbridge and Airdrie before turning south through Carluke and Lanark. Aside from stopping to sell goods at local markets, we would usually travel until just before sunset. Mr Lavery was well-acquainted with many of the people we met en route and most nights were spent under a roof. Our accommodation included barns, sheds and even a farmhouse just outside Lanark. On a few occasions, however, the tent was erected on the back of the cart and we all slept inside. As Goose had said, it was comfortable so long as there were not too many goods requiring storage out of the rain.

We arrived at Peebles on the Friday before the beginning of the Beltane Fair. On the Saturday Mr Lavery took Goose and me across the river where we saw a man dressed in a long, red coat with white and blue trimmings and a strange triangular hat, standing at the Mercat Cross, where he proclaimed the opening of the Fair to the large crowd that had assembled. This signalled whoops and shouts from the crowd, which then rapidly dispersed. Most of the men made directly for the taverns, while the women and children wandered amongst the stalls and booths that lined both sides of the main street. After we had returned to the cart and loaded our baskets with goods, we set off around the taverns selling as much as we could before all the money was spent on drink. Mrs Lavery, with Annie and Peter in tow, concentrated her selling efforts on the women and children. As the day wore on, the male population, in particular but not exclusively, became more and more boisterous. About mid-afternoon we all met up and made our way back over the river to the cart. After a very good supper of stew and potatoes, Mrs Lavery produced some scones and some cream cakes that she had purchased from one of the stalls. Despite our full bellies, we children fell upon these treats as though we hadn't eaten for days. After the meal, Mr Lavery erected the tent long before the sun was due to set. As this was unusual, I asked him the reason.

"Annie and I will be going across to the street dance this evening, so I'm just making sure that you youngsters will be able to get to sleep, as we will be late back."

Although my, by-now legendary, curiosity demanded to see the dance with my own eyes, I held my tongue and accepted that it was obviously not a place for children. Shortly before sunset, we were put to bed before they left to go back across the river. The music had started about an hour before and, as darkness fell, the music and the accompanying whoops from the dancers could be heard much clearer in the still, night air. Our cart and all the others were situated in a field on the south bank of the river. When we looked out of the end of the tent at the rear of the cart, we could see all the lanterns in the streets on the other side. I found it impossible to sleep and whispered to Goose that I wished that we could have gone too.

"Wait till Annie and Peter have gone to sleep and I'll show you something. Bring your spyglass with you" he whispered in reply.

On hearing this, any thought of sleep was driven even further from my mind. After what seemed to be an interminable wait, first Peter then Annie drifted off to sleep. Goose got up and started pulling on his boots. I followed his lead immediately, stopping only to retrieve my spyglass from my jacket. We crept out of the tent and jumped down off the cart. Sandy, who was tethered to the rear of the cart, eyed us curiously before returning his attention to the grass below him. We made our way down the bank until we reached the river's edge. Goose pointed to the slopes of the opposite bank. As there was a full moon, the bank was bathed in the softness of the moon's light reflecting on the water. At differing distances along the slopes, I could see what looked like bodies and, as my eyes became accustomed to the limited light, I could see that they were wearing very little clothing, if any at all.

"What's happening, Goose?"

"They're making babies," he replied with a broad grin. "Give us a loan of your spyglass."

I gave him the spyglass and he held to his eye and slowly scanned the length of the bank before handing it back to me.

"Here, Willie, have a look. You can see some of their bits."

178

Wondering what he meant by "their bits" I held the spyglass to my eye and I soon found out. As well as the sight of the rising and falling of several pairs of buttocks, white in the moon's light, I was also rewarded with views of women's breasts and other private parts, both male and female.

"Good stuff isn't Willie," Goose asked still grinning broadly.

I mumbled a reply which I hoped would reflect a mutual enthusiasm but, in reality, I was still too young to be stirred by what I had seen and I also felt a little guilty and ashamed. After using the spyglass a few more times, we made our way back to the cart and settled down to sleep. This would be only the first of the many occasions that I would encounter the sight of almost-public intercourse taking place as we made our way round the various fairs and festivals. As a result, by the time I returned home, I was fully acquainted with the rudiments of procreation but, not yet, the inclination to play any sort of active role.

At first light on Sunday, I was awakened by a gentle shake from Mr Lavery whilst everyone else was still asleep. He motioned me out of the tent as he held my boots and jacket. When I reached the edge of the cart, he lifted me down and told me to put my boots and jacket on. In spite of my confusion about what was going on, I did as he told me. When I was ready, he took me by the hand and we began walking across the bridge and into the town. As we were walking along the street passing the odd body of one of the previous night's revellers sleeping off the effects of the drink, I asked him where we were going.

179

"It's Sunday and you've got Mass to go to."

In all the excitement of the travelling, bargaining and other activities, I had, in all honesty, forgotten about Sunday Mass.

"Is the chapel near here?"

"Oh. There's no chapel but there's always a priest who comes to the town to hear confessions and celebrate the Mass, because a lot of the travellers are Catholics."

I imagined that, if last night's sights were anything to go by, the priest was going to have a busy morning. About two thirds of the way along the street, we crossed over and made our way down a narrow lane and into a large field. A small tent had been erected and there was a queue of mostly men, but with some women, outside. I thought that, if this was the confessional, then a lot of the men must have been with local women the night before.

Other people were standing about laughing and joking as they waited for the priest to finish absolving the sinners and to come out and start the Mass at the makeshift altar, on which the candles had already been lit, and which had been set up about twenty feet from the tent. Mr Lavery knew many of the people and seemed to be at great pains to assure them that he was only there because of me, in response to the good-humoured remarks about his return to the fold. When the Mass was finished, everyone said their farewells and expressed their hopes that they would soon meet again at the forthcoming fairs. By the time we got back to the cart, everyone else was awake and dressed and we all had a breakfast of salted porridge, washed down with strong tea, before everything was readied and we set off for Galashiels. My trip to Mass was to be repeated every Sunday during all the weeks we were travelling. Sometimes the Mass would be held in a real chapel, but mostly it was in a field or a barn and I became very friendly with many of the children, whose families seemed to follow the same itinerary as us.

Chapter Twenty Three

Scraps and Traps

We spent only one night in Galashiels before heading south to St Boswell's. As we approached the town, I remarked on the two high, steep hills, which dominated the landscape. The other hills on our route had been lower and more rounded.

"If you think those are high, wait till you see the mountains when we head north," said Goose in reply to my comments. "Sometimes you can't see the tops of them because they are covered in clouds."

I thought to myself that he was giving himself over to his usual exaggeration, since these hills were the largest I had ever seen and I had no concept of mountains having spent all of my life within the confines of the city.

When we reached the town itself, I was astounded by the variety of carts and caravans assembled around the green. Even Mr Lavery's cart, with all its decoration, couldn't stand comparison with the highly-decorated caravans, which seemed to be more like houses on wheels. The people living in them spoke a language that I didn't understand. Mrs Lavery and, to a lesser extent, her husband, were soon engaged in conversation with many of the caravan dwellers. It transpired that these were Gypsy people, who had travelled north from England and

Wales. On the way, they had purchased a great deal of crockery in Staffordshire and it was from them that the Laverys bought the stock that they would use for hawking back home.

During the three days that we spent there, we children were left to our own devices, as there was no selling to be done. While Goose's mother was engaged in fortune-telling alongside the Gypsy women, his father was taking part in the boxing matches inside a large tent. On one or two occasions, Goose and I abandoned Annie and Peter and crawled under the side of the tent to watch some of the fights. I saw Mr Lavery fight five men, one after another. These men were locals, who had accepted the challenge to fight with a ten-shilling reward if they lasted for three rounds. Most of them lasted less than two or three minutes before being carried out semi-conscious to make way for the next fool. This was also when I got my first taste of real toe-to-toe battle. Goose, being Goose, tended to open his mouth before thinking and this became the source of not a little conflict. Gypsy boys, in particular, were very quick to take offence at the most innocent of remarks and some of the stuff that Goose said was far from innocent. As a result, we were involved in at least three fights on a daily basis. I tried to put the skills I had been taught into practice, but after being on the receiving end of few beatings, I realised that I still had a lot to learn. Goose fared somewhat better, but, generally, the black eyes, bruises and split lips were shared on a more or less equal basis. If I had appeared at home looking as I did, my mother would, most probably, have had a fit, but Mr Lavery just laughed and advised us to keep our guard up in future. Similarly, Mrs Lavery's only response was to

183

give us pennies to hold against the swelling and damp cloths to wipe off the blood. As the days and weeks passed, we couldn't and didn't avoid regular fights wherever we travelled. As advised, I kept my guard up and, slowly but surely, I found that I was able to give as good as I got. Sometimes we would actually fight on the same side as the Gypsies when they were picked on by the locals. These fights were particularly vicious, because we were usually outnumbered and it was not unknown for some of the Gypsy girls to also get stuck in. On one occasion, in Perthshire, I was pinned to the ground by two boys, when one of them let out a yell and ran away closely followed by his pal. As I got up, I noticed Annie holding a heavy, iron pot in both hands and grinning from ear to ear. Fighting seemed to be a way of life for the Gypsies, even amongst themselves. It didn't seem to matter if you won or lost. If we stood and fought we were given respect and, while we would never be accepted as a part of the Gypsy community, we would certainly be regarded as being worthy of their friendship.

On the morning we were leaving St Boswell's, the rain came. Although the tent was still in place, all of us, except for Peter and Mr Lavery, had to get off the cart until it could be driven off the grass and on to the more solid surface of the dirt road. When we got back on, we were soaked through. We took turns undressing behind a blanket being held up by Mrs Lavery. We wrapped ourselves in the dry blankets she gave us and we all turned our backs while she did likewise. Soon we were all huddled together, trying to keep warm. Unfortunately, the rain didn't stop for nearly two days and, because of the lack of shelter on the ground, this meant that we had to eat

184

cold food, although, when possible, Mr Lavery would light a fire in the shelter of a large tree so that he could give us something hot to drink.

The rain stopped on the morning we arrived in Musselburgh, which brought me a whole new experience. As the sky cleared, the sun shone down and gave me my first-ever glimpse of the sea. My wonder at the sight must have been written all over my face, because of the comments being made by the others. I turned around to face them, still open-mouthed.

"Would you youngsters like to go down and play on the beach while we get the cart sorted out?" Mr Lavery said to our disappearing rears, as we rushed out of the tent.

"Take Peter with you," called Mrs Lafferty to no-one in particular. As far as Goose and I were concerned, her remark was aimed at Annie, as we two continued in our headlong rush towards the water, blankets streaming in our wake. Still holding the blankets around us, we ran into the shallow water and started to splash around, kicking water at each other. Although the water was very cold, it was a lot less uncomfortable than being soaked by rain. Some of the water went into my mouth and I reacted to its saltiness by spitting it out again and continued to spit using my own saliva to rinse out the aftertaste. Annie, still wrapped in her blanket was standing ankle-deep at the water's edge, but Peter, naked as the day he was born, was happily splashing about. He fell into the water completely on several occasions, but seemed to have the instinct to keep his mouth closed and wait until he surfaced before drawing breath. As a result, he was probably having a lot more fun than the rest of us. After about half an hour, we were called back to the cart. We took turns, once again, of drying off and dressing behind the blanket before settling down to our breakfast porridge, the first hot meal we had had in days.

Later in the morning, we travelled through Musselburgh, stopping only to buy some fish before journeying on to Portobello, where we spent the night. The next morning we did some selling in the local market, but by midday we were off again as Mr Lavery wanted to avoid a night in Edinburgh, since that might cause a problem with the Peelers. As we travelled through the city, Mr Lavery pointed out the castle sitting atop a rock which seemed as high as the hills at St Boswell's and another high hill that he told me was called Arthur's Seat, after King Arthur, about whom I knew nothing until Mr Lavery, as usual, related his version of the story of the king and his knights.

After spending the night on the outskirts of Edinburgh, we journeyed on until we reached a small village called Kirkliston. Although it was well before sunset, Mr Lavery drove the cart into a farmyard, where we were warmly welcomed by the farmer, Mr Murray, and his wife who, it transpired, was the sister of Goose's uncle Duncan. Although we had to sleep in the barn, we were treated to a substantial meal in the farmhouse proper, where we were joined by the Murrays' three grown-up sons. After the meal, the sons left to continue their work on the farm before last light, while Mrs Lavery and Annie took Peter, who was falling asleep, off to the barn, accompanied by Mrs Murray, who wanted to have "a wee blether". Goose and I sat with the two men as they chatted about things that had happened since they had last met the previous summer. Since I was obviously a new face, Mr Lavery explained who I was and why I was travelling with them. He then added that I was one of the most curious people he had ever met.

"It's getting to the stage that I'm scared to tell him anything, as I know that he's going to come out with endless questions. Why, just yesterday, I showed him Arthur's Seat and then had to spend the next twenty minutes explaining about Arthur and his knights," he said jokingly.

"Och. There's nothing the matter with a boy asking questions. That's the only way he's ever going to learn anything. If my boys had never asked me anything then they wouldn't be much use to me on the farm."

Then, turning to face me directly, he continued.

"Hundreds of years ago, there used to be knights here as well when the village was called Temple Liston. They built the first church before it was burned down and the new Kirk was built."

"Were they King Arthur's knights?" I asked.

"No. They were long after King Arthur and they were called Templar Knights."

"What are Templar Knights?"

"I see what you mean." This was said to Mr Lavery before he told me what he knew about the Templar Knights. In reality, he did not know very much, but because of my continual questioning, it took him quite a long time to finish telling me the little he knew. He seemed a little relieved when he managed to bring the story to an end and, when he saw that Mr Lavery and Goose were struggling to contain their laughter he quipped.

"I'll not make that mistake again." Then he joined in the gales of laughter now released by Goose and his father.

At first light the following morning, we made our usual preparations for leaving before having a porridge breakfast with the Murrays in their house. Mrs Murray wrapped a large amount of bread and cheese in a cloth and gave it to Mrs Lavery before we left. Mr Murray filled our two tins with fresh milk and handed them to Goose, who was already on the cart. After handshakes all round and hugs from Mrs Murray, we set off to make our way through the village proper and take the road for Bo'ness.

We reached our destination just as night was falling and we had to hurry to set up camp and have our evening meal before it became too dark. This was made all the more difficult because of the number of carts and caravans that were already there. It was quite late, therefore, before we could all settle down, but the lateness helped me to fall asleep almost immediately instead of laying awake for ages, as I normally did.

As we were having breakfast the following morning, I heard the sound of a band playing in the distance. Mr Lavery got up immediately, swallowed his tea, un-tethered Sandy and led him away.

"He has to take Sandy to the stable before the parade gets here," said Goose anticipating my query.

Before I could ask my next question, he explained that his father would be driving in the horse and trap race in the afternoon and that it would be impossible to get through the parade. I thought it very amusing to imagine Sandy being in a race, given that I had only ever seen him move at a plodding pace. What I found out, later in the day, was that all the other horses taking part were working horses too. Thoroughbreds for the gentry, but good, honest, working horses for the miners of Bo'ness.

We watched the parade as it passed us at Corbiehall and carried on out to Kinneil House, where all the men were given whisky to drink. I thought it must have been very strong whisky as many of the marchers seemed quite drunk as the parade returned and made its way through the town but, as was more probably the case, there had been a more substantial intake from the jars that many of the men were carrying. Goose and I helped Mrs Lavery to set up her small fortune-telling booth before heading off to find his father. Annie, dragging Peter by the hand, came with us, in spite of Goose's objections. We had some difficulty reaching the stables as the streets were still full of people, many of them already at the staggering stage. When we eventually arrived, we found that Mr Lavery had washed and brushed the horse down and was now braiding the hairs of his mane. He set us to work, cleaning and polishing the trap, which we had passed on the way in. The trap belonged to a friend of his who didn't like to use his own horse in the race. When all the cleaning was done, Sandy was hitched to the trap and Mr Lavery led him down to the banks of the river with all of us following behind. There were a few others already there having practice runs along the course. Mr Lavery led Sandy to the starting line and motioned us to stand aside. As we moved to do as he had indicated he said.

"Not you, Goose. You have work to do."

Goose's face was crestfallen as he wondered what other task he would have to carry out, but this was immediately replaced by a broad grin when his father continued.

"You're old enough and ugly enough to be keeping up the family name, so you're doing the driving today. Now up you get."

Goose was so excited about being given the honour that he fell off the trap while trying to climb up too quickly.

"That's not a very good start, is it?" Annie ventured and even Goose joined with the ensuing laughter.

Following his second, more successful, attempt to mount the trap, Goose had four runs at the course at increasing speeds. When the practice was finished, it was Goose who led the horse to the trough before we all returned to the stable. While waiting for the races to start, we all sat outside the stable having our midday meal of bread and cheese that we had brought with us, washed down with water from the river. As we ate, we watched the locals as they staggered around. Mr Lavery said that the evening dance in the Town Hall would be sure to end in the usual mass brawl. When I asked if he and Mrs Lavery would be going, he replied that he had made that mistake some years ago and had not been minded to repeat it since.

The afternoon races started with a trap race in which Goose didn't do very well. The next race was a carriage race for double teams of horses. Goose did a little better in the third race and, following the next carriage race, managed an honourable fourth place in the final trap race. The last race of the afternoon was for the pit ponies, ridden by the miners' children. I noticed that Annie was crying silently while this race was taking place.

"It's not fair, Willie. Those wee ponies are kept under the ground and working all the time. It's all right for the men to get a holiday but the poor wee ponies are still made to run up and down."

"They're just animals and that's what they're there for," I thought to myself but I remained silent so as not to upset her any further. However, to my surprise, her father indicated his agreement with her.

"You're dead right, Annie. But I'm afraid that it's just the way of the world. At least they are getting the sun on their backs for a change."

Unfortunately, his remarks were not sufficient to stop her tears but she hugged herself to him in response to the sympathy with which they had been delivered.

Chapter Twenty Four

The Summer Walkers

The next day, we set off on the short journey to Grangemouth, where we stopped to spend the day with Goose's auntie Peggy and the Donaldson family on their boat, which was moored on the Forth and Clyde Canal. When I got on to the boat, I was quickly reminded of Goose's remark about how tiny the living cabin was. How so many people could live in such a small space was incredible, even to me who had experienced the crowded living conditions in the Wynds. I suppose that, given that the main purpose of the canal boats was to transport cargo, it was understandable that space would be at a premium and living quarters would, necessarily, be a secondary priority. The Donaldsons, however, seemed totally at ease with the situation and, somewhat miraculously, made room for all of us to sit and eat, although we had to retreat to the cart at night.

After wishing a fond farewell to the Donaldsons, we set off early next morning and, over the next few weeks, we travelled on through Falkirk, Stirling – which also had a castle atop a high rock; Alloa, Dunfermline and Kirkcaldy which was memorable for its long street market and the constant, acrid odours emanating from the linoleum factories. Mr Lavery knew a wealth of information about the history of all the places we passed through and communicated this knowledge to all of us, even at the risk of triggering my inevitable questions. About two miles outside Kirkcaldy we stopped at a field just outside the small village of East Wemyss. Mr Lavery sat silently on the cart while his wife, Goose and Annie went into a field. Goose turned around and gestured for me to follow. We walked over towards a large oak tree and stopped about five feet from it. Mrs Lavery had been picking some of the wild flowers from the field as we walked and she formed them into a little posy and laid it on the ground. She then said some words in the language I had heard her using at St Boswell's.

"She's praying for my wee sister I was telling you about," Goose whispered.

I decided that I would say a wee prayer for her as well but I did so silently. However, without thinking, I joined my hands, as I had been trained to do by the nuns when saying my prayers and was caught in the act by Mrs Lavery, who had turned to face us. I could see tears in her eyes and, when she saw me standing with my hands joined, they began to flow more freely although she had a broad smile on her face. She didn't say a word as she gave me a short, but tender, hug then walked back towards the road with us following.

"Thanks for that, Willie," Goose said, his voice breaking and, for the first time ever, it was *I* who put my arm round *his* shoulders in a gesture of sympathy.

We travelled the next few miles in silence, but it did not take long for Mr Lavery to find another point of interest to tell us about.

Our journeys took us to St Andrews, Cupar, Kinross, Perth and Crieff. It was in the latter town that I first met the Summer Walkers. This was the name given to the Highland travellers. They, too, spoke a language that I did not understand and that Goose's parents could only speak a little. They did not live in caravans and had few carts. They seemed to carry most of their belongings on their backs or on the backs of ponies. They lived in tents shaped like a bow, but they tended to be involved in the same activities as the other travellers we had met to the south. At night, they gathered in large groups around their fires and told stories, sometimes breaking into song. Mr Lavery told me that their songs also told stories and that that was their way of preserving the history of their families and of their culture. He said that all of them could name all of their ancestors going back for hundreds of years. As my knowledge of my own earliest ancestor consisted only of my father's grandfather, I envied them this knowledge and wished that I, too, could know more about my background. When I mentioned this to him, he told me that I should find out as much as I could from my grandparents.

"If you don't find out, how are you going to be able to tell your own children? It's important that *you* know and that you let *them* know where and who they came from, because where and who you come from is what makes you what you are."

After Crieff, we travelled towards Lochearnhead. As we made our way there, I marvelled at the size of the loch and the surrounding hills and mountains. I had seen the large loch in Kinross, but Loch Earn seemed to be so much larger, nestled as it was amongst the high ground. As well as having a productive selling day, we all enjoyed the sights of the Highland Games that were taking place and which also involved the surrounding areas from Balquhidder and Strathyre. Men were tossing cabers, great tree trunks which must have been at least twice the size of the men themselves, hammers and large stones. There was also a lot of music, singing and dancing. Apparently the games had started as a way for clan warriors to practise their battle skills and to improve their strength. I assume that the singing and dancing must have reflected the celebrations that took place when the enemy had been vanquished.

It was also in Lochearnhead that I nearly drowned. As it was a hot day, Goose and I joined many other children in splashing about in the cold waters of the loch. As we were playing, I took a step and put my foot down on nothing but water. Losing my balance I fell over and down into the water and started to sink in spite of my best efforts to regain my footing. What I didn't know was that the water was only shallow around the edges and that there was a steep drop continuing the slope of the hill. After what seemed like an eternity, I felt a hand gripping my hair and I was pulled to the surface by a man whose name I did not know, but whom I recognised as one of the Summer Walkers we had met in Crieff. He spoke to me in his own language then changed to English.

"You are a very lucky boy. Many people have drowned in this loch and you were nearly one of them. You should ask your father to teach you to swim if you intend to play in the water."

As I stuttered my thanks he walked away with just a short wave of dismissal. As I recovered, Goose arrived with his father whom he had gone to fetch when he saw my predicament.

"Are you all right, Willie," Mr Lavery asked breathlessly, having run all the way from the games field. Before I could answer he continued. "Right. That's it you're all going to learn how to swim or you'll not be going near the water again."

Although I didn't care if I never played in water again, he decided that the lessons would start there and then in spite of our protests and, from then on, he took every opportunity he could to continue with our instruction so that, before we returned to Glasgow, all of us were capable swimmers. Peter, in particular, had no fear of the water and he could soon swim like a fish.

Later, I mentioned to Mr Lavery that the man who had rescued me had spoken to me in English but he had sounded more like the nuns than like the ordinary people I met on a daily basis.

"That's because his natural language is Gaelic which used to be the language that everybody spoke in Scotland and in Ireland and Wales for that matter. So, when he learned English, it was like learning a foreign language which meant that he learned the educated version. What we speak is a different sort of English. Even different parts of England speak different sorts of English, but everybody understands the educated sort."

When our sojourn in Lochearnhead came to an end, we set off towards Crianlarich, stopping frequently to cut white heather. It was this white heather that Mrs Lavery sold in the dockside pubs and door-to-door and which most people regarded as being lucky. After passing through Crianlarich, we made our way south on the west shore of Loch Lomond, which was much larger than even Loch Earn. When we reached the village of Tarbet, Mr Lavery steered the cart on to a road on our right and towards the west. This road was extremely hilly, but, no matter how high the road, we were always dwarfed by the high mountains on either side. After about two miles, we arrived at the village of Arrochar, which was situated at the head of another large loch. I learned that this loch, Loch Long, was different from the others I had seen, since it consisted of sea water, as opposed to the fresh water contained in the others. We purchased a large amount of mussels, which we put into all our spare buckets, along with water from the loch to maintain their freshness. Before retracing our route back to Tarbet, we all had a meal of mussels, after they had been boiled in fresh water in the large cooking pot over the fire. They did not look appetising in the slightest, but my experience with the sheep brains gave me the confidence to try a taste and I wasn't disappointed. They were absolutely delicious and left me with a life-long fondness for mussels and other seafood.

As we made our way back over the undulating hilly road, Mr Lavery gave me another history lesson.

"Remember I was telling you about my Viking ancestors?"

"The ones that conquered all the countries?"

"That's them. Well they used to sail their ships up to where Arrochar is now, then they would drag them over the hills to Tarbet, put them into the water of Loch Lomond, then sail around all the villages on the banks of the loch and attack them."

When he talked about ships, I imagined the ships I regularly saw at the docks and I thought that he must be setting me up for another joke. However, he, seeing the incredulous look on my face continued.

"You look as though you don't believe me."

"Well, I think it would be impossible for somebody to drag a big ship with all those masts and sails over this wee road."

"They weren't those types of ships. They were more like really long versions of the rowing boats that you see up at our end of the river, but it still wasn't easy for them because this road wasn't even here at the time."

I still found it hard to believe and spent the remaining time until Tarbet waiting for the others to start laughing and expose my naivety, but they never did.

We spent the night in Tarbet in the company of a good number of Summer Walkers, but I did not see the man who had saved me. The next day, we continued south through Inverbeg and Luss, until we arrived at Balloch and made our preparations for the Fair, which would take place the following day. We made our camp beside all the other travellers on the

198

south edge of Balloch Moss, where the stalls and booths were being set up. While we helped Mrs Lavery to set up her fortune-telling tent, her husband went off to make arrangements for some boxing. The Fair started very early the next morning. As we children had the day to ourselves, we spent our time wandering around all the different stalls. Goose and I attempted to crawl under the side of the boxing tent to watch his father. Fortunately for me, he was the first to go under and, therefore, the one who was caught by a man whose job it was to catch the non-payers and who ejected Goose with an accompanying kick in the arse.

We left the showground and walked up to the Horse Fair, which was just as entertaining, with all the negotiations and arguments that were taking place. If I thought that I had any skill as a negotiator, it paled in comparison with the activities of the horse-traders as they conducted their business and sealed their deals with a spit on the palm of their hand and a firm handshake. Many of the traders were Summer Walkers who were selling off their surplus ponies before heading home to the Highlands. Balloch was the farthest south that the Summer Walkers travelled, since the Fair took place in September and they had to get back to their winter quarters before the first snows. We, however, were not under any such pressure, as was evident when we spent the following day in Balloch instead of packing up and leaving, as most of the others had done. This also gave Mr Lavery time to recover from the previous day's exertions. His fights had started just before noon and his last had taken place well into the late evening and early night by the light of paraffin lamps.

Our penultimate day of travelling took us through the Vale of Leven and Dumbarton to the small village of Bowling. Mr Lavery showed me the canal and told me that this was the other end of the Forth and Clyde Canal that I had seen at Grangemouth. He also told me about the Antonine Wall that the Romans had built as a defence against the natives and which also started over at Bo'ness and finished at Bowling. When I asked him where the wall was, he told me that it wasn't a proper wall, like Hadrian's Wall down at the border, but more of a continuous high ridge made of soil and turf and that most of it was long gone. Before the day was over, the poor man found himself having to give me a potted history of the Romans and the Celts. In spite of his seeming exasperation at my continual questioning, I think he was secretly glad that I was interested enough to seek more information and I, to this day, am grateful that he took the time and had the patience to impart much of his wide knowledge. I also believe that my admiration for his seemingly endless store of knowledge, not to mention the numerous books that he found for me to read, together with a dictionary that I could use to "look up the hard words", is what inspired me to take every opportunity through the years to expand my own learning

We arrived in Glasgow on the Saturday afternoon. As we had come in on the Dumbarton road, we detoured through the docks, but only to check if there was anything to pick up. However, the Belfast boat had gone and there were no cotton ships in port, so we negotiated our way across the now-completed tramways and through the evening traffic until we reached the Laverys' house in the Saltmarket. We, very quickly, unloaded the cart so that Mr Lavery could get to the stables before darkness fell. Goose suggested that I should stay for the night and his mother said I could if I wanted to, but I would still have to get up early the next morning to get home and join my mother and grandmother before going to Mass. Although I was desperate to see my family again, I decided that I would stay and I spent my last night with the Laverys in the welcome comfort of a soft bed in the company of Goose and Annie.

Chapter Twenty Five

"It's the man"

I was awakened early on the Sunday morning by Mr Lavery. Unfortunately, this also meant disturbing Annie and Goose. The latter, in particular, was not best pleased about his sleep being brought to a premature end, but, after some brief, muttered complaints, he was soon his usual cheerful self. When we went through to the other room, we had a quick wash in some cold water before putting our clothes on as rapidly as possible, since the fire had only recently been lit and the house was still cold. When washing, we all remarked on the sight of the viaduct outside the window. The brickwork looked as if it was nearing completion and it seemed to be within touching distance of the window. When Mr Lavery took me downstairs to return me to my mother, we could see the skeleton of a bridge across the Saltmarket. We had not noticed this the previous evening as it was above the level of the gaslights on the street. This sight served only to confirm how close the railway would pass to the Laverys' house, given that the bridge seemed to be an extension of the building itself.

"Are you looking forward to seeing the trains going past the window, Mr Lavery?" I asked excitedly.

"To be quite honest, Willie, I'm not sure that we'll be there very long once the trains start. Our building has seen better days and I don't think it will last much longer with all the vibration there's going to be."

"But we saw lots of railways and trains when we were travelling and there were houses all around them and they didn't fall down."

"Maybe so, but they weren't as close as our building is and they were also in much better condition, but we'll wait and see. Anyway, are you looking forward to seeing your ma and your granny again? I wonder if they'll recognise you."

As I replied that I was and that I was also looking forward to telling them about all the places I had been, I was puzzled as to why he wondered if they would recognise me as I had only been away for three months. What I didn't realise was that I had grown a good two inches and that I had put on quite a bit of weight, mostly muscle, due to the good food I had been eating and the physical work I had been doing. In addition, my skin had been browned by the sun and I had lost the normal grey pallor of the slum-dweller.

When we arrived at my grandmother's house after negotiating our way through all the new construction works, which had left the area almost unrecognisable, I ran up the stairs and into the house, leaving Mr Lavery to follow at a normal pace. My entrance startled my grandmother who was sitting in my grandfather's old chair and who did, indeed, take a few seconds to recognise me.

"Oh, Willie. You gave me such a start. Well, won't you look at you all grown up and as brown as a berry."

"Where's my ma?" I asked, noticing that she wasn't in the room. When I hadn't seen her when entering, I had assumed that she was still asleep, but the bed was empty.

"Oh. Your ma? Ehm, your ma went to visit your uncle Liam yesterday and she must have stayed the night." As she said this, Mr Lavery knocked on the open door and asked if it was alright for him to come in. She welcomed him warmly and offered him a cup of tea from the pot which was sitting on the range.

"If you don't mind, Lizzie, I'll have to get back as Annie will have my breakfast waiting. We just thought that we should get Willie back in time to go to Mass with his ma and yourself."

"That's very good of you, Ben. Willie, would you get changed into your Sunday clothes while I see Ben out?"

As I moved to do as she had told me, dreading that my mother would return having been informed about James' mishap, she went outside with Mr Lavery and I heard them conversing in a low voice. I could not make out what they were saying, but I am certain that I heard my grandmother's voice almost breaking, though I thought nothing of it at the time. What was of more concern to me was the fact that my Sunday clothes no longer fitted me. My jacket was just a bit tight but the bottoms of my short trousers were almost at my groin. When my grandmother saw this, the somewhat sad look on her face was replaced by a smile and then laughter.

"My God, Willie, you haven't half grown. We can't have you going to chapel like that. Get yourself under the bed and fetch me my sewing box."

As I retrieved her box, she found an old pair of my grandfather's trousers amongst the clothes that she had kept, even though he was now nearly two years dead.

"I'll cut these down and make them into a pair of shorts for you."

"But there's not enough time. We'll be late or we'll have to go to St Alphonsus' instead" I protested.

At my mention of St Alphonsus', her face fell and I thought it must be because of the reminder of my grandfather's death.

"We'll not be late and we won't be going to St Alphonsus'"

As it transpired, she was as good as her word and we managed to get into the chapel just as the priest was coming on to the altar, although we had to sit with the men at the back. I was glad that we sat there because my shorts were not the best example of my grandmother's handiwork, given the haste in which she had made them. Being at the back also meant that we were among the first out and I could avoid anyone I knew as we returned to Back Wynd.

My mother had still not returned from my uncle Liam's by the time I had changed my clothes and had breakfast, so I asked my grandmother if I could go out to play. She told me not to go too far as my mother would probably be home soon. I went down to Osborne Street to have a good look at the works.

Directly in front of the Wynds, there was the beginning of a large building. It had high brick walls supporting iron girders which would hold the roof. I assumed that this would be the railway station. All of the area to the south of the building had been dug up and then flattened. I could make out the route of the railway, although there were, as yet, no rails laid. It came in over the river and then split. One branch headed off towards Goose's house, but the main part made a sweeping curve around the back of a church towards Stockwell Street and the massive bridge that had been built across it. When my eyes followed the line of the curve, I could see a much bigger building under construction near where the Theatre Royal had been. This was, in fact, the St Enoch's station and Hotel. The building I had assumed to be the station, would be the sheds where all the maintenance would be done on the engines. As there were no fences around the site, I was able to cross over and join a lot of other children who were already playing there. To my surprise, I didn't know any of them, so I decided to have a wander round and have a good look at the works. My sight-seeing was brought to an abrupt end by an angry voice which came from the direction of the worker's camp, situated over by the viaduct, which would carry the railway up to Goose's house.

"Get yourselves to fuck out of there or youse'll get my boot up your arses."

"It's the man" cried a few of the children as they ran back towards Osborne Street, with me following close behind.

By the time my grandmother came out to call me in for my dinner, my mother had still not returned. We were just finishing our meal of stew and potatoes when my mother came in. When she saw me, she threw her arms wide open.

"Oh, Willie. You're home. When did you come back? Did you have a good time? Did you miss your mammy?"

I rushed into her arms and held her tightly, my reply muffled due to my face being flush against her chest which, like the rest of her, had a strange, yet vaguely-familiar, stale smell.. As my joy was replaced by trepidation about what she may have been told, I asked her how my auntie Lizzie was.

"I was telling Willie how you had gone to visit our Liam," my grandmother interjected as my mother hesitated in her reply.

"Oh your auntie Lizzie's fine and so's your uncle Liam and your cousins. They were all asking for you. Now come on and tell me all about your trip"

I was relieved that James had managed to keep his mouth shut and I wondered how my auntie Lizzie had failed to notice his socks. However, all of these thoughts were banished as I recounted some of the stories of my trip with the Laverys. I judged it prudent to keep some of the more exciting, but less salubrious items to myself.

Although my grandmother had kept some food for my mother, I was surprised when my mother said that she wasn't very hungry and that she felt a little tired and that she needed "a wee lie down". My grandmother looked angry and ready to say something, but any remark was forestalled by a knocking at the door. I opened the door and was faced by Goose's smiling face.

"You coming out, Willie?"

Before I could answer, my grandmother told me to go out and play for a while. I snatched my jacket and cap, said my goodbyes and sped out. As I was running down the stairs, I could hear the raised voices of my mother and grandmother through the open door although, because of my headlong rush down the stairs, I couldn't catch the gist of what sounded like an argument.

"I wonder what they're arguing about," I said to Goose.

In return, he gave me a strange look and seemed to stop himself from saying something in reply. Instead, he suggested that we head up to the Britannia to see if we could get in. Unfortunately, the doors were closed, so we had to make do with sitting outside and listening.

"My da says that we're not going out tomorrow because he's got a few people to see."

"Do you want to come with us to see your uncle Peter when we go for my granny's stuff tomorrow?"

"What time?"

"We usually leave about six, so we could meet you at the Cross about five, ten past."

"Fuck that, Willie. You already spoiled my long lie this morning and I'm going to make up for it tomorrow."

Although disappointed that he wouldn't be joining us and surprised about his wanting "a long lie", given that he was usually the first up and always bright and breezy in the mornings, I accepted his excuse and I moved the conversation on to reliving our adventures on the road. As darkness fell, we split up. Goose went through the alley into the Trongate, while I made my way back down past Waxy's to my grandmother's house. As I made my way up the stairs, I could, yet again, hear the sounds of an argument, which stopped as soon as I opened the door. For the rest of that evening, all seemed normal, although I could still feel the tension in the room, which lasted all the way until bedtime.

The next morning, my mother and I rose early and made our way towards the Gallowgate. Despite Goose's insistence that he was going to stay in his bed, I searched the Cross with my eyes in the forlorn hope that he had changed his mind. If only he had, then my blissful ignorance would not have been shattered by the news that my mother was about to give me.

"Willie, son, I think I should tell you that I've met a nice man. His name is Declan Walsh and he is working over on the railway. His wife is dead and he has a wee girl called Catherine, who is seven and they live in New Street. I've told him all about you and he is looking forward to meeting you. In fact, you'll see him later today when he comes to your granny's for his soup."

"What the fuck?" I thought to myself. If she had told me that she was going to buy a long black dress and join the nuns, I would have been less surprised. As it was, I maintained my silence as I tried to digest this astounding information. When my father had died, I had assumed, erroneously as it turned out, that the three of us would continue to live together as a family until I met a girl, got married and started a family of my own. Declan Walsh, or any other man, was not part of the plan.

"Are you not going to say anything son? Are you not happy for your mammy? You'll like Declan and Catherine, I promise."

In reply I told her that I could not understand why she would need anyone else when she had me and my grandmother.

"I wasn't looking for anyone else. It just happened and you've got to remember that I'm still only thirty-two, so I've got a good bit of my life in front of me."

I didn't tell her that, in my eyes, thirty-two was quite old; too old, in fact, to be going with another man. As we continued along the Gallowgate in silence, I assumed that the arguments the previous day must have been about my mother and this Declan Walsh. I was soon to find out that my assumption, while not completely mistaken, was far from being totally accurate.

The rest of the morning was spent preparing and cooking the food for the midday meal for the workers. My mother had told my grandmother that she had told me the news, in answer to the first question she heard as we went into the house. Apart from that brief conversation, they hardly exchanged a word before the first workers began to arrive. For almost an hour, we were busy filling and refilling bowls, as well as doling out other food. Although the men only had thirty minutes for their break, the break was split, so that only half of the men were off at any one time. It was during the second thirty minutes that I was introduced to Declan Walsh.

"Willie, this is Mr Walsh" my mother said, smiling up at the tall man who had an arm around her waist.

"Pleased to meet you," I said, hoping that my face did not display the fact that I would have been as pleased to meet a ghost on a dark night.

"And it's pleased to meet you as well. Mary Ann you didn't tell me what a fine figure of a fellow your boy was. Sure isn't he almost as big as a man already?"

"He is indeed, Declan," my mother replied, still smiling, still looking up at his face.

"I hope you will be remembering how to make this fine soup when you come to live with us."

"Oh yes. I meant to tell you, Willie. Declan's house has got two rooms and we've agreed that it would be a good idea if we went to live there. Just think, you and Catherine will have a room all to yourselves."

That was it. All semblance of calm and acquiescence on my part was shattered along with the empty bowl that I had been holding and which I threw to the floor, before squeezing past all the workers and escaping down the stairs, ignoring my mother's shouts to "come back this minute" and her threats of retribution if I didn't obey her at once. I kept running and didn't stop until I reached Goose's house in Saltmarket. With propriety forgotten, I entered without knocking, and ran to Mrs Lavery, crying uncontrollably as she held me to her.

"I take it he must have heard about the man." I heard Mr Lavery say.

Chapter Twenty Six

Relocation and Fornication

As it transpired, the Laverys knew all about my mother's new man, as he had been the subject of my grandmother's conversation with Mr Lavery which had taken place on the stairs after he had brought me home. I also became aware that my mother's absence, ascribed to a visit to my uncle Liam, had, in reality, been an overnight stay at Declan Walsh's house in New Street. As New Street was situated behind St Alphonsus' chapel, then the reason for my grandmother's reluctance to go to that chapel also became clear. Rather than bringing back memories of my grandfather's death, it had been to avoid the possibility of any unexplained encounter with my mother. As Goose probably knew about the situation as well, this would have been a more plausible reason for his reluctance to accompany us to the slaughterhouse that morning.

Although Goose's parents were sympathetic and endeavoured to comfort me in my distress, they were also adamant that I must return home and obey the wishes of my mother.

"But I don't want to move away from my granny and I won't be able to come and work with you." I protested.

"Nonsense. Your granny will still need you to get her stuff from our Peter, so you'll still be down here in the mornings and we can pick you up. It's not as if you're moving to the other side of the world; it's only to the Calton after all. Besides, you have to do what your ma tells you and that's that."

By his response, it was evident that I would have no support from that quarter in any defiance of my mother. Utterly defeated and despondent, I was escorted back home by Goose and his mother. As we went up the stairs to my house, we could hear my grandmother and my mother arguing inside. Rather than allowing me to continue inside, Mrs Lavery held my hand while giving a loud knock on the door. Immediately, the raised voices were silenced and the door was opened by my mother.

"Oh thank God. I was hoping that he had come round to you. We were so worried after he ran away. Thanks for bringing him home, Annie."

"Not at all, Mary Ann. I think he was just a wee bit confused and upset, but he's all better now. Isn't that right, Willie?"

I nodded in meek response, but I ignored my mother's proffered hands and walked over to my grandmother instead. Mrs Lavery declined my mother's offer of a cup of tea, citing her need to collect Annie from school and I was abandoned to my fate. For the rest of the day, hardly a word was spoken and I was glad when bedtime arrived and that sleep arrived to banish the events of the day.

The next morning, in spite of my stated wish to go to the market on my own, my mother insisted on accompanying me. On the numerous occasions that she tried to engage me in conversation, my grudging response, if any, consisted of a curt "yes" or "no". Although I had no idea at the time, so consumed as I was with self-pity, my rebuttal of my mother's attempts to rebuild her bond with me must have hurt her deeply. I did not realise that my coldness and my grandmother's obvious disapproval served only to isolate her from her blood family and make her even more emotionally dependent on Declan Walsh. As far as I was concerned, my tactics of near silence were successful, since she never again accompanied me to the market. Paradoxically, the lack of support from the Laverys seemed only to strengthen my bonds with them. Their insistence on my obedience to my mother was, after all, nothing but a confirmation of the status quo. It was expected that children should obey their parents and, deep inside, I knew that there had never been any chance, whatsoever, that they would support me in defying my own mother. In my mind, they and my grandmother were the constants and it was my mother who was letting me down.

On my return from the hawking on Friday, my mother informed me that we would be moving when Declan finished his shift the next day and that I should have all my things ready before I left for the docks in the morning. After a meal of leftover soup and bread, I left the table and gathered my clothes, wrapping them in a knotted sheet. At one point, my mother went out to speak to a neighbour and I took the opportunity to ask my grandmother to hold on to my pouch for me.

"Of course I will, Willie. And another thing. Don't you be getting upset about me and your ma falling out. It's only because I didn't want to be on my own again. I'm sure that everything will work out fine for you and your ma. Besides, I'm still going to see you every day just the same."

"I know, granny." I said lying through my teeth, as I was sure she had done. I had been able to piece together too many broken parts of their numerous quarrels to be left in any doubt that my granny was of the opinion that what she was doing was wrong, for my mother and for me.

Saturday seemed to pass in a flash and, almost before I knew it, the time came for my relocation. After leaving the Laverys, I returned to my grandmother's house and found my mother and Declan Walsh sitting with everything ready to go. All my mother and I had to carry were our clothes and a few ornaments. Everything else we had brought from Old Wynd was to be left behind, including Wolfe, as the Walshes' landlord did not allow dogs to be kept in the house. As we left, there was only the briefest of goodbyes shared by my mother, grandmother and Declan Walsh. I, on the other hand, was kissed and hugged warmly, handed some money and reminded to fetch the supplies from the market on the Monday.

Although it only took twenty minutes for us to reach New Street, it seemed like hours to me as I listened to my mother's excited chatter and the less-excited responses from her new man. When we arrived at number 23, we entered a close which, to my surprise was lit by gas lamps fixed two-thirds of the way up the walls. The Walshes' house was to the right on the ground floor and it, too, was brightly lit as I saw when the door was opened. When we made our way inside, a little girl ran to Declan Walsh and he picked her up and turned to me.

"Willie, this is Catherine and she's going to be your new sister. And, Catherine, this is Willie and he's going to be your big brother. Now isn't that going to be grand?"

Catherine, obviously, thought that it was, indeed, grand as she extricated herself from her father's arms and came over and cuddled me. I did not think that it was grand at all. As far as I was concerned *my* sisters were with my grandfather. However, despite my misgivings, I found her enthusiasm and obvious affection difficult to resist. After all, as nothing of this was her fault, it didn't hurt to give her a little hug in return. I was then introduced to Mrs Boyle, Declan Walsh's widowed sister, who lived upstairs and who looked after Catherine during the day. Mrs Boyle was one of the fattest women I had ever seen. Her head, topped by grey hair tied in a tight bun, seemed like an onion placed on top of a giant football which had two pudgy arms and two feet, the toes of which barely peeked out below the hem of a voluminous skirt, added as a sort of afterthought. Notwithstanding my unkind thoughts on her appearance, Mrs Boyle was, in fact, an extremely pleasant person and welcomed me warmly.

After being taken into the other room that I would be sharing with Catherine and unpacking my meagre belongings, I rejoined my mother and my new family as we had a meal of warmed-up soup, cold meat and potatoes. Shortly afterwards, Mrs Boyle returned and I learned that she would be looking after Catherine and me as my mother and Declan, as I had been invited to call him, were going out for the evening. After they had gone and Catherine had been put to bed, I sat with Mrs Boyle or Auntie Maggie as Catherine called her, and answered all of her seemingly endless questions about me. I thought that she was very nosy to be asking me all the things that she did, not realising that she was really trying to put me at my ease by engaging me in conversation about subjects familiar to me. As it was, I found it relaxing to tell her about some, but not all, of the activities in which I had been involved. She seemed particularly interested in my experiences on my travels and expressed her envy at my having been to so many different places. It transpired that, since coming to Glasgow from Ireland as a girl of fifteen, she had never once been outside the grim surroundings of the city which, for most common people at that time, was the norm. I warmed to her so quickly and enjoyed chatting to her so much, that I was disappointed when the time came for me to go to bed.

After I had climbed into bed, careful not to awaken Catherine, I tried my best to get off to sleep. However, owing to the unfamiliarity of the surroundings and my reawakened memories of my travelling, I found it impossible to fall asleep. After a few hours of struggle, any chance of achieving sleep was knocked on the head by the return of Declan and my mother. Owing to the loudness of their conversation it was apparent that they had been drinking. Fortunately, my mother's usual propensity to start arguing when she had been drinking did not manifest itself. Instead, I heard them both thanking Mrs Boyle and saying goodnight before they settled down and continued talking. After a few minutes, everything went quiet and I assumed that they had

217

gone to bed. As the realisation was dawning on me that the stale odour that I had smelled on my mother had been the same one that I used to smell on my father the day after he had been drinking, I heard other sounds emanating from the other room. These were sounds that I recognised from the many occasions when Goose and I made illicit use of my spyglass and I wondered how long it would be before my new family had a new addition. I also speculated on how long it would be before some priest would come calling to deliver a similar message as had been delivered to Granda Willie and Auntie Hannah. After an almost sleepless night, I arose and put on my Sunday clothes. I had just finished dressing when my mother came in and wakened Catherine. As she was helping Catherine to get dressed, I went through to the other room where I gave my face a perfunctory wash in the sink, which was fitted with a water tap. The noise of the running water must have disturbed Declan, who had still been asleep when I entered the room.

"Ah, it's yourself Willie. Did you have a good sleep?"

I gave a falsely enthusiastic "yes, thank you" in reply and sat down to put my boots on.

"Where are you off to?" he enquired.

"Are you forgetting it's Sunday, Declan?" This from my mother who had entered the room with Catherine.

"Sunday?" he replied with a puzzled look. "Ah yes Sunday. Well I'd better be getting up and be getting ready. Wouldn't want to be late for chapel."

About ten minutes later, Mrs Boyle came in after a brief knock on the door.

"Is Catherine ready for chapel yet?" She asked.

"We're all ready." My mother replied rather quickly.

The short look of confusion on Mrs Boyle's face and Declan's puzzled response to my informing him that it was Sunday, were sufficient evidence for me to reach the conclusion that going to chapel had not been part of the plan for that day. This was further borne out by their almost furtive entry to St Alphonsus' and by their failure to take Holy Communion. If their activities at the end of the previous night were to continue then, I concluded, this was a situation which was not likely to change in the near future and may well have been one of the wrongs that my grandmother had argued about with my mother.

This charade, however, lasted just three weeks, after which only Mrs Boyle, Catherine and I continued to fulfil our Sunday obligation. Also, despite our proximity to the chapel, no priest ever came, no ultimatum promising hellfire and damnation was delivered and no marriage between my mother and Declan ever took place. Thankfully neither was there any new addition to my new family, despite the best, almost-nightly efforts of Declan and my mother.

Chapter Twenty Seven

Singing for the Suppers

Much to my surprise, I adapted to my new situation reasonably quickly. One advantage of living in New Street was that I didn't have so far to travel to buy my grandmother's supplies. Since my mother was now responsible for taking Catherine to school, I continued to carry out this task on my own, which, if truth be told, was a situation that suited me fine. The bond between my mother and me had been severely weakened and would never be the same again. I still felt that she had betrayed me and, despite her best efforts, I could never bring myself to return the affection that she continued to show me. My grandmother's relationship with my mother never recovered either and, during the period when my mother continued to help her in the food business, any mention of her life in New Street was answered with a frosty silence and a grimace of disapproval. I have often heard it said that the Irish ability to remember slight, offence or perceived wrong, would put an elephant's memory to shame. My own experience leaves me in no doubt of the probable veracity of this statement, but the consequences of a lack of forgiveness can be grave and I am certain that the attitude shown by my grandmother and me played a large part in influencing my mother's future behaviour. Whilst some might excuse my treatment of my mother, due to my relative lack of years and maturity, I will carry my feeling of guilt and shame until the day I die.

Although my weekdays continued to follow their usual course, I found new work on a Saturday. Mr Lavery had heard that Owen 'Tomato' Gorman had died and suggested that Goose and I should step in and take over his fruit business, as Annie was now old enough to be left on her own on the cart with Peter down at the docks. Never having met Tomato Gorman, I had visions of Goose and me pushing a handcart around the streets and selling fruit. However, when I started to ask questions about the elements in my imaginings, everyone started laughing. At first I thought that I had been set up again and waited to hear what the joke was.

"You've got the wrong end of the stick, Willie. Tomato Gorman only sold rotten fruit, mostly tomatoes, and he didn't sell them round the streets." Mr Lavery explained. "He sold the fruit in the singing saloons in the Saltmarket."

It transpired that the singing saloons, which were mostly situated on the eastern side of the Saltmarket, were miniature versions of the Britannia. Although there were the usual drinking areas as in other pubs, a section would be set aside and long benches fitted so that the men and some women who paid their penny could be entertained by singers and comics. Since not all of the entertainers were of a particularly high standard, the audience would show their disapproval by booing and pelting the turns with rotten fruit, which they had bought from Tomato Gorman and which they would now be buying from us. Mr Lavery also told us that we would be working for ourselves.

"I'll give you any money you need to get started and you can pay me back, but anything above that you keep. Just remember that you will have to pay the owner to let you sell in his pub, but the harder you work, the more you'll make and the more you'll keep. And don't, under any circumstances, attempt to cheat anyone, as the consequences will be painful if you're caught."

The last part of his statement was accompanied by a stern look aimed directly at Goose, who didn't even blush.

So it was that Goose and I became involved in the retail fruit business. On Saturday mornings, we would go to the fruit market and fill our baskets with all the discarded soft fruit that we could find. On occasion, there would not be enough to fill our baskets and we would have to buy from the traders, but, since it was near the end of their trading day, we could normally buy at a good price We carried our baskets on yokes that Mr Lavery had made for us to the same design that he had used for his own. I thoroughly enjoyed my new occupation, as did Goose. We soon familiarised ourselves with the layout of all of the different establishments. This was no easy task as it was extremely difficult to distinguish much due to the clouds of thick smoke being generated by all the drinkers. After a few weeks, we were firmly established. We now knew all the owners and had made the necessary financial arrangements with them and we were able to find our way to the entertainment sections with no trouble at all. On a good day, Goose and I could make as much as four shillings each after everyone else had been paid.

It was about three months in to our endeavour when Goose revealed another hidden talent. We were in the Sun Tavern at the time, when a singer came on who was so bad that Goose threw a tomato before anyone else could. The singer, seeing that the tomato had been thrown by a young boy rather than by a grown man, decided to take exception to his action and made towards Goose. He was stopped by the men in the front row and started to protest.

"What right has a wee boy got to be throwing tomatoes at a grown up?"

"Because you're fucking rubbish." Goose replied and everyone started laughing.

"If you think you can do any better, then come up here and do it," the singer retorted, his voice raised to overcome the sounds of laughter.

"Right, I will," said Goose cockily and the audience's laughter increased, although there were also some shouts of encouragement.

"Oh no," I thought to myself. "He's really done it now."

However, he was a revelation. He had the voice of an angel and when he gave a rendition of an old Irish ballad telling of the loneliness of being in a land far from home he brought the audience, some of whom threw coppers on the stage, to its feet. The singer had made a furtive exit after the first verse and Goose had the stage to himself. He did not need much encouragement to sing two more similar songs especially when he saw the coppers at his feet and, when he left the stage, he was loudly cheered and was almost floored by the slaps he took to his back.

Goose became a regular turn in all the saloons and was more than adept at judging his audience. Most pubs were predominantly Irish, but a few were patronised by mostly Scottish people and he would choose his repertoire accordingly. The 'singing' money was added to our fruit money and the profits were split evenly between us so that we managed to make an average of six shillings each every Saturday.

The pubs we frequented were rough and mirrored the living conditions of their customers. They were crowded, smoky and dangerous when fists and missiles started to be thrown, an occurrence which took place several times daily in every establishment. The rear outside walls were commonly known as 'pishing walls', as they were the locations used by customers to relieve themselves. However, no matter how accustomed I had become at some of the sights I had seen over the years, nothing could have prepared me for what I witnessed in the aptly-named Odd Fellows tavern.

Goose was on stage singing and I was standing at the end of the back row having made my sales. I noticed a woman getting up from the far end of the second row and making her way, unsteadily, to the space between the back row and the wall. To my utter astonishment, she bunched up her skirts, squatted and began to pish into the sawdust which covered the floor. As she finished, she gave out an audible fart, shook her hips, straightened up, smoothed her skirts and made her way back to her seat. I almost couldn't believe my own eyes, but the wet patch in the sawdust was enough to prove that I had not imagined the whole thing. It was as I was looking at the wet patch that I noticed that there were several discoloured patches all over the floor at the back. Seeing all of these patches I imagined that, either other women used this area for a similar purpose, or it was the one woman with a weak bladder and a fondness for drinking too much.

To safeguard our interest during our summer travelling, we made an arrangement with John Mulgrew, of whistling and cap-thieving fame, and his cousin, Peter, by which they would operate our fruit business on the understanding that we would take over again when we returned. Their understanding, being somewhat different from our understanding, necessitated a degree of physical violence on our part to successfully reclaim our business and to ensure that normality was resumed.

As that year drew to a close, the railway work came to an end and the trains were now running regularly. The magnificent St Enoch's Station and Hotel were now completed and were in full operation. Anytime that I was in Goose's house when a train passed, reminded me of Mr Lavery's previously-stated misgivings. The whole building seemed to shake and it was not uncommon for some of the ceiling plaster to fall to the floor, via the body of anyone unfortunate to be standing underneath. Thankfully, however, no-one was hurt and the building, in defiance of its age and condition, remained standing.

Unfortunately, the structure of my home life fared rather worse. Declan had to travel out to Lanarkshire to find work after the railway was completed. As I was away for most of the day and Catherine was at school, my mother was left on her own for long intervals and descended into a melancholic loneliness, which, allied to my and my grandmother's distinct lack of affection, pushed her towards her finding solace in another direction and she started to drink heavily. On numerous occasions, I would come home and find her slumped in a chair, while Catherine would be upstairs with Mrs Boyle. If the situation was unpleasant for me, it must have been ten times worse for the wee girl. She did, indeed, regard me as her big brother and, consequently, she thought that I should play with her all the time. Tired as I usually was after working all day, I found it impossible to refuse her as she was such a thoroughly-likable child. In addition, as my mother's alcohol-induced stupors became more and more frequent, Catherine began to cling to me even more and my only relief came with the occasional return of her father. Declan, however, was far from happy when he found out about my mother's behaviour, which he no doubt heard about from his sister and from Catherine's excited ramblings.

The resultant arguments between Declan and my mother could clearly be heard by Catherine and me in the bed we shared and she would cuddle into me for comfort as she trembled at the sound of angry voices. Not once, however, did I ever hear Declan use violence against my mother, even though I knew that she was not above raising her hand to him. I wondered how long this situation would continue before Declan lost his patience and kicked us out and we would have to find another place to live. Little did I know that I would soon be living in a very different place but not with my mother and certainly not through any choice on my part.

Chapter Twenty Eight

Robbery and Assault

That Saturday, which would prove to be so pivotal in my life, was as any normal Saturday. Goose and I had carried out our business and were heading back to his house when he suggested that we should go into the Musical Tavern, which was in the same close as the Shakespeare Tavern, to try and gather a few extra coppers by way of his singing. After he had sung three songs, we gathered up the coins and went out into the close, where we were greeted by the sound of a woman's muffled screams. As we peered through the gloom, we could see that there was a woman lying on the ground and a man was on top of her. His left hand was covering her mouth while his right hand was busy beneath her skirts. Without hesitation we ran to assist her and I caught the man on the head with a well-aimed kick. As he fell over, Goose gave him a few more kicks and he passed out. We helped the woman, who was obviously drunk, to her feet and she thanked us before staggering into the Shakespeare. I started to walk away down the close, but Goose, true to form, decided to rifle the man's pockets. As he was busy searching the man's pockets he was interrupted by a shout from the close entrance where, to my horror, two Peelers had appeared. As Goose made to run off, one of his hands was stuck in a pocket and he was felled by a truncheon which one of the Peelers had sent spinning through the air. I ran back to help him but the other Peeler cracked me on the left shoulder, before a well-practised blow to the head rendered me unconscious. When I came to, lying on the ground beside Goose, I found my hands cuffed and blood pouring over my face from a large gash on my head. The Peelers dragged us out to the Saltmarket, where one of them stood guard while the other went back up the close to speak to the man. However, he returned almost immediately to say that the man had gone. Goose attempted to explain about the attack on the woman but, since we had interrupted the attack before the man had opened his trousers, the Peelers would only have seen Goose rifling the pockets of an unconscious victim and Goose's attempt at an explanation was answered with a kick and he was ordered to keep his mouth shut.

We were dragged down to the jail at the bottom of the Saltmarket, searched and relieved of our money, un-cuffed and thrown into a large cell which was already crowded with all manner of miscreants who had been arrested between Friday and Saturday.

"Willie, when they ask us our names, you say that you're William Lavery and I'll say that I'm Isaac McCart, that we're cousins and that we're both thirteen. When they ask us where we live we'll tell them we have no fixed abode and, whatever you do, don't tell them that you are a Catholic. Just say 'Presbyterian'"

He went on to explain that, if we gave our correct names and addresses, the Peelers might raid our houses and that could cause a major problem for his father. When I asked him why we had to hide the fact that we were Catholics, he replied. "Two reasons. First of all, Catholics get treated worse than Protestants. Secondly, if we get put away, the last thing we want is to end up with the priests or brothers, as I have heard that there are some right funny buggers amongst them."

Bowing to his superior wisdom, I did as he had told me and thus it was that William Lavery and Isaac McCart appeared before Baillie James Thomson, magistrate and sometime butcher, on the Monday morning. We were charged with assault, robbery and vagrancy. Since we had admitted that we had no fixed abode we pled guilty to the vagrancy charge and not guilty to the others. The two Peelers gave their evidence and stated that they had recovered nine pence from me and one shilling and four pence halfpenny from Goose. The thieving bastards had pocketed the rest of our takings from the day. Since we did not think that the magistrate would believe in our chivalrous intentions any more than the Peelers had, we simply denied having been involved in any assault or robbery. After some deliberation, Baillie Thomson gave his verdicts. On the charge of assault he pronounced the 'bastard' verdict of not proven since there had been no witness to the assault and the victim had not come forward. We were both found guilty of robbery based on the 'eye-witness' accounts of the Peelers, who swore that both of us were observed to be rifling the 'victim's' pockets.

Before sentencing us he enquired about our ages and religious persuasion and, after being informed that we were both thirteen years old and Protestant, he ordered that we be taken to the North Prison in Duke Street, where we would each receive twelve stripes of the birch. After this punishment, we were to be transported to Slatefield Industrial School, where we would be put to productive work at the rope-making until we reached the age of sixteen. He finished by saying that he hoped that the school experience would be beneficial to us and that we would leave the school reformed and ready to restart our lives as upright citizens. We were then taken down to the cells to await our transport to the prison, whilst the trials continued in the courts upstairs. While we waited, we were surprised by a visit from Mr Lavery, who had slipped a couple of shillings to the gaoler. Our arrest had not gone unnoticed and he had been informed of our predicament upon his return from the docks. When word spread of our arrest, it did not take long for the locals to tie in the circumstances of our arrest with the ravings of a drunken woman recounting her salvation at the hands of two young boys. As a result, as we were expecting Mr Lavery to blow his top at our getting ourselves arrested, we were surprised when he told us that he knew the whole story. When we told him that the Peelers had stolen most of our money, he simply shrugged and told us that that was nothing unusual and continued.

"You two look after each other when you're inside. Keep your heads down and avoid trouble if you can, but don't take any messing about from the other boys. I'll try to visit you when I can as your 'Uncle Ben'. Willie, I've told your granny what happened and she's going to tell your ma. If I can, I'll bring your ma with me as your 'Auntie Mary' when I'm visiting. And, just to let you both know, that I'm so proud of you for what you did." As he said this, his voice began to break and tears came to his eyes as he said his goodbyes and left.

When the time came for our transportation to the prison, we were manacled along with about eight other prisoners, led outside and made to climb up into a black carriage which had bars in the window spaces on the sides and on the door. The carriage rattled swiftly over the cobbles and after only fifteen minutes we heard the prison gates close behind us. The carriage door was opened and we descended into the courtyard. I had seen the outside of the prison on many occasions and I recognised the pungent odour emanating from the Molendinar Burn, which passed through a tunnel beneath the prison yard and reappeared at the other side of Duke Street beside the chemical works and the tannery. However, the view from inside the walls was radically different. The buildings looked so tall, dark and forbidding and I was thankful that I would soon be leaving this place, although I was dreading the coming punishment. The other prisoners were led away whilst Goose and I were pushed through a door and into a badly-lit room, where I first caught sight of the birching table.

The guard who had pushed us in joined another guard who was already standing there. We were un-cuffed and told to sit on a bench against the wall. In the corner; I could see three large jars which had handles of bound twigs protruding from their openings. After a few minutes, a well-dressed man and another man in shirt-sleeves entered the room. The well-dressed man was the doctor, who was supposed to ensure that the prisoners' capability to endure the punishment was regularly checked. If, in his opinion, further punishment would cause serious damage to a prisoner's health, then he was duty-bound to call a halt. The other man's role was to mete out the proscribed punishment. Since we were both under fourteen, our punishment was limited to a maximum of twelve strokes. Fourteens and over could be given a maximum of thirty-six strokes. Since Goose was almost fifteen, his foresight seemed to have saved him from a worse punishment. Also, if he had stated his true age, then no-one would have believed that I was thirteen (which was true) since I was two to three inches taller than he was.

Goose was called up first. He was stripped from the waist down and made to lie on the table with his arms inserted in two holes so that they dangled freely below the table. His privates fitted into another hole which had a bucket underneath. His waist was secured by a strap and his feet were bound together and secured to the table by another strap. His head was turned towards me and I could not believe my eyes when he winked at me. The man who was to administer the punishment selected a bound-bunch of twigs from one of the jars. I noticed that there was water dripping from the twigs. This water was, in fact, brine and was used to keep the twigs supple and to act as an antiseptic for any cuts. In reality, all the brine did was to add weight to the twigs and exacerbate the punishment.

As the man approached the table he had a quick look underneath and laughed.

"Look at that little dickie. I've seen a bigger one on a new-born baby." The other men laughed with him.

"Funny that," replied Goose, "your daughter told me it was bigger than yours" The laughter from the other men grew louder while the man's face grew a bright red and he lifted a balled-fist to strike Goose on the face before regaining his control.

"Fucksake, Goose. You've done it now. Why can't you keep your mouth shut?" I said to myself.

"Right then. Twelve strokes it is," said the man as he raised the birch and used all of his power to deliver a heavy blow to Goose's buttocks.

"One....two...three."

He continued counting strokes until he reached eleven.

"What was it you were saying about my daughter, funny man?"

Goose who had, until this time not uttered a sound, replied

"I said that she said that my cock was bigger than yours. Oh and by the way, your wife and mother said the same thing."

"Oh right, I *thought* it was something like that. Now where was I? Ah yes, I remember. Three...four...five." He continued with the birching and as he reached 'nine' again, I saw Goose's eyes close as he passed out and let go of a stream of piss into the bucket below. The doctor did not intervene and the birching continued till Goose had received a total of twenty-one strokes. Still unconscious, he was roughly removed from the table and I could see that the cuts extended from his thighs to his waist. The two guards put his trousers on him and then he was dropped to the floor.

When it was my turn, I am not ashamed to admit that my fortitude was somewhat less that that displayed by Goose. After the first stroke, I screamed and I lost control of my bladder and by the fourth stroke I was only semi-conscious, although I did not pass out altogether. I believe I was also fortunate because the man's arm must have been tired after the effort expended in delivering Goose's punishment.

When my punishment was completed, I was released from the table and ordered to get dressed. As I did so, I noticed that Goose had regained consciousness and was putting his boots on. As he bent over to tie his laces he winked at me again. Once more, I was astounded. I could not believe that he had suffered almost twice the pain that I had and here he was, still defiant, whilst I was in total agony. We were manacled once more and led back out to the carriage which had brought us. As the carriage left the prison for our journey onwards, every bump of the wheels on the uneven cobbles was conveyed through the body of the carriage and exacerbated the pain in my lower regions. This torture was almost as unbearable as the birching I had received and I was glad when the carriage stopped and we were taken out and deposited in the entrance hall of Slatefield School. With hindsight, perhaps a more appropriate term would have been "the entrance to the hell of Slatefield School".

Chapter Twenty Nine

The Rope Walk

Goose and I were ordered to wait while the guard walked off to find someone who would take charge of us. I looked around at the cold and forbidding surroundings of the entrance hall and, almost immediately, my eyes rested on a large wooden sign above the door at the other end of the hall and my heart sank as I read:

"There will be sustained quietness and instantaneous obedience."

Memories of my first school came flooding back and I was filled with even more trepidation than that which had gripped me since the beginning of the day. Goose must have noticed a change in my expression and whispered a few words of encouragement.

"Don't worry, Willie. It'll be just like any other school except that we'll have to do a bit of work as well. We've already taken the best that these bastards can give us and we're still standing. All we have to do is what my da told us. We'll look after each other, keep our heads down and knock fuck out of anybody that tries to mess us about."

I found little comfort in Goose's encouragement, after having witnessed his goading of the bircher. If that was his idea of keeping his head down, then our stay at Slatefield was certain to be eventful.

My thoughts were interrupted when a door opened and the guard returned with another uniformed man and a man wearing a smart suit. The guard left and we were ordered to follow the other two men through the same door that they had used. This door led to a small room with two doors. We were ushered through the door to our right and found ourselves in a room which had tiles on all four walls and was furnished with a chair in the centre of the room and a table in the corner. We were ordered to take off all of our clothes and our boots. While we stood, naked, the uniformed man threw our clothes into a basket, but put our boots on the table in the corner. Goose was instructed to sit on the chair and, after he did so, the uniformed man cut all of his hair off using a set of clippers that he had produced from his pocket. It did not take long before I suffered the same fate and, as I caught sight of my red curls lying on the floor, I was consumed with sadness at the re-awakened memories of my grandfather. When the shearing was finished, we had to stand in a corner of the room where we were sprayed with a jet of freezing-cold water by our erstwhile barber and then, still dripping wet, were ordered through yet another door.

"Sustained quietness" was not what we encountered as we entered a long, high hall. To our surprise and embarrassment, we were subjected to a stream of barracking, hoots and catcalls from all the boys who were sitting at the long tables which lined both sides of the hall, and who were, evidently, having their evening meal. Our faces glowing with

236

embarrassment and our hands endeavouring to cover our modesty, we were forced to walk down the middle of the hall until we arrived at a door in the far end. When through this door, we were each given a shirt, short trousers, pants and socks, all coloured black, and ordered to dress. We were also given our own boots but since they too had been sprayed with water, we were told to carry them until they dried. The smartly-dressed man, who, by now, was seated behind a large desk, motioned to us to stand before him.

"My name is Mr McNaughton and I am the governor of this establishment. This gentleman here," he continued, pointing to the uniformed man, "is Mr Wilson. You will soon be acquainted with all of the other members of staff, but, as far as you are concerned, Mr Wilson and I are the most important people in this school. At all times, you will obey all rules, or you will suffer the consequences which, I assure you, will be dire in the extreme. All male members of staff will be addressed as "sir" and all female members of staff will be addressed as "miss", except for Matron Wilson, who will be addressed as "Matron". You will learn all the other rules from your dormitory leaders, but I give you fair warning that you had better learn them timeously, as ignorance will not be accepted as an excuse for the breach of any rule whatsoever. Do you understand me?"

"Yes, sir," I was first to reply.

"Yes, sir," echoed Goose, much to my relief.

Mr Wilson ordered us to go back into the hall, where we found that all the boys were finishing their meal in total silence. We were to learn that all meals were normally taken in silence. It was only when new boys arrived that this silence was allowed, in truth, encouraged, to be broken as a means of disheartening the new arrivals. As embarrassed as I was by my welcome, I can only imagine how much worse it must have been for some, poor lad having to face such treatment on his own. We had to stand, unfed, while the others finished their meal. All of the plates and cutlery were gathered by a few of the boys and taken away to be cleaned. Some boys were tasked with sweeping up, whilst others were washing the tables. It transpired that all of the work in the school, from peeling potatoes to polishing the floors, was all carried out by the inmates. Some of the "housework" tasks excused the participants from any rope-making activities and were highly-prized.

Mr Wilson called over two of the older boys and told them to show us to our dormitories.

"Lavery, you go with Fleming here," he ordered, indicating the slightly-taller of the two, "and, McCart, you're with Smith."

Goose and I almost forgot that we had exchanged names but we managed to avoid making any obvious mistake and did as we were ordered. This was our introduction to the leaders of the Fleming and Smith, "Smiddy", gangs. They were not gangs in the sense that they fought with each other. I suppose they were more akin to fraternities, although the treatment meted out to the younger members, in particular, was far from brotherly.

We all went out of the dining hall and ascended a large flight of stairs. At the top, I followed Fleming to the right, whilst Goose followed Smiddy to the left. The dormitory was about half the length of the hall below and was lined with wooden beds on either side. Fleming showed me to a bed on which was a rolled-up, thin tick mattress, a bare pillow and a blanket.

"So, Lavery, what are you in for?"

"Robbery, sir," I replied.

"Don't fucking "sir" me. I'm not one of those bastards. I'm stuck in here the same as you for another three months anyway. Now, here are the rules. No talking during the meals or during school. You can talk during the work but if you stop your work to talk then you'll get hammered. You can talk after your supper, but not in the dormitories. You just get into your bed and get to sleep. If you pish the bed you'll get hammered and you'll have to sleep on the boards till your mattress is washed, because there are no spares. Before you go to bed you have to wash your feet and, when you get up in the morning, you have to wash your head. Do you get all that?"

When I said that I understood he added:

"Whatever you do, try not to be on your own with that fucker, McNaughton. What colour's your hair?"

When I told him that my hair, when I had some, was red, he told me that McNaughton preferred boys with fair hair. In my relative innocence I imagined that Goose would have the advantage on me when his hair grew back in. Just then, the dormitory started filling up with other boys and Fleming told me to make up my bed, take off my shirt and socks and make my way to the wash room, which was at the far end of the dormitory.

The wash room consisted of two long metal troughs, back-to-back and situated in the middle of the room and with water taps every five or six feet down their length. Facing one side of the troughs was a tiled channel, which the boys used to piss in. On the opposite side, was a bench arrangement with holes cut at regular intervals. There was a small pile of torn newspaper beside each hole, which needed no further explanation as to its purpose, as the odours emanating from the holes overpowered even the carbolic smell which seemed to pervade the rest of the washroom. I did as everyone else did and washed my face and hands in the cold water before lifting each foot, in turn, and subjecting them to the same treatment. All of these ablutions were carried out in total silence and this silence persisted as everyone went back into the dormitory and got into bed. After the gaslights in the dormitory were turned off, I lay awake for some time unable to sleep due to the residual pain from the birching and to thoughts of everything else that had happened that day and of what the days that were to follow might bring.

The next morning, I was awakened by Fleming's shouts for everyone to get up. Again I followed the example of everyone else, including holding my head under the flow of the water tap, and got ready for what the day would bring. We had a meagre breakfast of thin porridge, the first food I had eaten since Saturday morning, and cold water to drink before those fortunate enough to have secured housework tasks, all of whom were older boys, went off to carry them out, whilst the remainder were split into dormitory groups. That week was our dormitory's week for morning rope-work, whilst the other dormitory had morning school. The system changed on a weekly basis such that the following week I would have morning school and afternoon rope-work. It was not difficult for me to catch a sight of Goose as he followed the others towards the door which led to the classrooms, as he was one of the few boys whose head was bereft of hair. When our eyes met, he gave me a slight grin, which I returned in kind, being careful not to be observed by Wilson or the other staff members who were hovering around us.

Two of these staff members led us out of the school and down a steep path to a long building that I recognised as a rope walk having seen many such buildings where I lived. One of the staff members, Mr Watson, took eight of the older boys into the building whilst the rest of us were kept outside with Mr Kemp, who looked towards me and said:

"Lavery. You'll be starting out here hatchelling with these boys. If you work hard and keep your nose clean, you might get to work inside. Understand?"

"Yes, sir," I answered, meekly.

Hatchelling involved separating strands of hemp by drawing them through a hatchel, which was a board with long spikes driven into the base. This work was always done outside no matter what the weather and, in no time at all, my whole body, my hands and fingers, in particular, were excruciatingly cold. In addition the smell of the whale oil, which was used to help the strands run freely, made it

241

difficult but not impossible, thankfully, for me to keep down the porridge I had eaten at breakfast.

That first morning seemed to drag on forever and I was overjoyed when were taken back to the main building for our midday meal, which consisted of a thin soup and a plate of potatoes and cabbage. This was followed by thirty minutes of association when the silence could be broken and I could go and find my pal. When we got together, I told him about the work I had been doing and about the cold and the smell. When I said that I was glad that I would have school in the afternoon, he laughed and said:

"If you get the same teacher as me, you'll be wishing that you were back out there. His name's MacDonald and he's a fucking nutcase. I think he starts every class by picking a row and giving everybody in the row two of the strap, just to remind everybody about who's in charge. Then, during the class, I happened to look at him as he was looking at me and he gave me two for staring at him and another two for being insolent when I said that I hadn't been staring at him at all."

Before I could make any comment, our conversation was interrupted by Fleming and Smiddy, who informed us that we were not supposed to talk to anyone outside our own gang. Goose's protestation of "you must be fucking joking" was stifled by Smiddy's hand grasping his throat and threats of unwanted and painful retribution if he did not do as he was told and if he continued to act like "a cheeky wee bastard". In spite of these dire warnings, we endeavoured to talk whenever we could manage to slip away from the main group.

242

That afternoon, Goose's description of Mr MacDonald was proven to be true. I don't believe that my being in the row selected for the strap was entirely due to bad luck. Rather, I believe that the row was selected due to my bald head giving me away as a new inmate and, therefore, someone who would benefit from an early laying-down of the rules. Notwithstanding Mr MacDonald's disciplinary eccentricity, I found that I enjoyed his class. He very quickly noticed that my level of knowledge seemed to be greater than that of the other pupils and, consequently, would give me a book to read whilst he was busy with the rest of the class. At the beginning, one or two other members of the class took it upon themselves to take exception to what they regarded as preferential treatment, but after a few bouts of fisticuffs followed by the inevitable punishment, I was left in comparative peace. On one occasion, Mr MacDonald gave me a bible to read. Although I had heard a few of the stories before from the priests and the nuns, I was astounded and pleasantly surprised by the wealth of stories contained in the Old Testament. Many of the stories were better than those in the books that Mr Lavery had given me and I thought that those Israelites must have been a lot like the Irish, since they loved their God and their country so much, even though somebody else was always coming along, kicking their arses, and treating them like dirt.

Chapter Thirty

The Rape Walk

Bearing in mind what Mr Lavery had advised, I kept my head down and settled into the routine of the school and rope-making. In the early days, this routine also included regular sessions with the tawse, due to my fighting with older boys in response to their attempts to bully me. At times, I also stood up for some of the younger boys who were also being mistreated and, consequently, there was a noticeable decrease in bullying whenever I was around. By no means did I win all of the fights in which I was involved, but my willingness to keep fighting and my ability to inflict painful damage on my opponents, led to my being left alone. Goose, too, must have been regularly involved in brawls as there never seemed to be a day when his face wasn't marked in some way or another. Apart from the lottery of the row selection for the daily strapping, I was never strapped for any misdemeanour in the classroom. The other misdemeanours were punished by Mr Wilson, who would have the offender held down over a chair by two of his colleagues while he administered the required amount of strokes to the offender's bare buttocks. More serious misdemeanours, such as stealing or attempting to abscond, were punished by birching, although this was, technically, illegal and the only 'medical professional' who would be present was Matron

Wilson, his wife, whose cure for all ailments was a large dose of castor oil.

The school and rope-making went on from Mondays to Saturdays. On Sundays, all the boys and staff assembled in the dining hall which was laid out for church services, which were conducted by a local minister and consisted of prayers, scripture readings and a long sermon, before concluding with still more prayers. The best thing about this service, in my opinion, was that I didn't have to kneel down as I did when I went to chapel. At first, I felt guilty that I was missing Mass every Sunday but, as the weeks passed, I felt angry that God had abandoned me in this place and that it was *His* fault that I was missing Mass. After church, we were allowed an hour of association until the midday meal, during which we were allowed to talk. After the meal, we had to endure two hours of Sunday school, which consisted of lectures about other scripture readings. This was followed by another two hours of association.

Once a month we were allowed a family visit during the afternoon association. On the first such visit, Mr Lavery turned up, not with my mother, but with my grandmother. When she saw the disappointed look on my face, my grandmother seemed pained and I quickly thanked her for coming to see me. She asked me how I was doing and told me that she had had to give up the food selling since all the workers had now left. She was, however, managing to survive by living on the money she had made, supplemented by some sewing and dressmaking. She also told me that Wolfe was missing me, but that I shouldn't worry about him as she was taking him out for a walk every day. When I

245

asked about my mother, she told me that she hadn't been keeping very well and that maybe she would come and visit me the following month. It was after they had gone that Goose informed me of the truth as we huddled in an alcove out of sight of prying eyes. Apparently, his father had gone to New Street on the Saturday to make arrangements for my mother to accompany him the following day. When he arrived at Declan Walsh's house, it was Mrs Boyle who answered the door. When he explained the purpose of his visit, she took him into the house, where my mother was slumped, drunk on a chair. He had made no attempt to speak to my mother, but had, instead, gone round to my grandmother's house, explained the situation, and arranged for her to accompany him in my mother's place. In all my time at Slatefield, I never saw my mother. My only monthly visitors were my grandmother and Mrs Lavery, who claimed to be my aunt.

Weeks passed into months and the routine remained the same until, due to enough of the older boys attaining their sixteenth birthday, I escaped the freezing cold of the hatchelling and was promoted into the relative warmth of the rope walk. I soon became acquainted with the methods of production of rope. The strands, which had been separated by the boys outside, were fixed to hooks on an upright board and were spun into a yarn by boys holding the strands and walking backwards away from the board. The yarn was then wound on to large bobbins which were placed on spindles at one end of the rope walk. The yarn from four or five of these bobbins was attached to a former, which was pushed towards the other end of the building, while being rotated by the turning of a cranking handle. A top, which was like a bobbin with grooves in its sides, was inserted amongst the twists to maintain the tightness of the braided rope. For all intents and purposes, the rope walk was assisting in my rehabilitation and I was repaying my debt to society through my involvement in such a valuable production process. However, there was a darker side to the rope walk and it was one for which it had never been designed and one which would lead to a premature end to my time in Slatefield.

On a few occasions as I lay on my bed, trying to sleep, I saw Mr Wilson and Mr McNaughton enter the dormitory, waken one of the younger boys and take him out. Sometimes a boy would struggle, but he would be powerless to resist the overwhelming strength of the two grown men. After about an hour, the boy would return alone and get back into bed and his sobbing could be heard through the whole room. I soon found out that the other boys called this abduction "going for a walk" and that it involved the victim being taken over to the rope walk and being mistreated by Mr McNaughton. In my initial naivety, I imagined this mistreatment to consist of a strapping, but I was soon made aware of the type of abuse which was reputed to take place. I only found this out from talking with some of the other boys, as none of the victims dared to say a word about their ordeals.

One night, after I had been at Slatefield for about seven months, I was awakened by Fleming's successor, Dunlop, who was due to leave in a few days.

"Willie," he whispered, "Smiddy's just told me that your pal has "gone for a walk with Wilson and

McNaughton. If you want to go and help him then I'll not stand in your way. I'll be getting to fuck out of here in a couple of days anyway."

I jumped out of bed and put my clothes and my boots on and made my way to the side door which led to the rope walk. As I opened the door I saw a lantern being carried up the path towards the main building. I ducked back inside and squeezed myself into a gap between a large cupboard and a wall. When the door opened, Mr Wilson entered, turned left and made his way down to a door at the end of the corridor. When he had closed the door behind him, I went outside and ran down the path towards the rope walk, guided by a light that I could see in one of the windows. As I made to open the door at the bobbin end of the building, I heard a man's high-pitched scream followed by other screams that I recognised as Goose's. I threw open the door and rushed in. At the far end I could see Goose lying naked on the floor while McNaughton, his trouser round his ankles and his groin bleeding, was beating him with the cranking handle. I grabbed the nearest object I could find which was a hatchel and ran towards them shouting:

"Leave him alone you fucking bastard. I'm going to fucking kill you."

On hearing my voice, McNaughton turned towards me and swung the handle as I got within range. As he swung, I ducked and swung the hatchel I was holding at his face. However, he had overbalanced when he missed me and the hatchel stuck in his neck, which caused his blood to spout everywhere and he collapsed to the floor. Goose, meanwhile, was lying, groaning on the floor. He had a massive

248

gash on his head and his right arm and leg were obviously broken, as the bones were sticking through his flesh. He was still conscious but when I tried to move him, he almost passed out.

"Willie, I'm fucked. I think the bastard's killed me and just because I bit his cock off."

It was as he said this that I remembered the bleeding around McNaughton's groin and, when I looked at the floor beyond Goose's head, I could see what looked like the top couple of inches of a penis.

"You're going to be all right, Goose, and I don't think you'll have to worry about that fucker any more. I think I've done him in. Now come on and I'll help you up to the house."

"Willie, I've told you I'm fucked and I can't fucking move. If you've really done him in you'll be fucked too. You're going to have to get away because you're covered in blood. Untie my hands so that I can say that it was me that done him. Everybody knows that you're my pal and I'll make them think that you ran away because you were afraid that you would get the blame as well."

"But, Goose, I can't run away and leave you here," I protested with tears streaming down my face.

"You'll have to. If we both get done they'll say we planned it and we'll get hanged. At least, if I last, I can try and say that I killed him in self-defence. You get away right now but don't go on the streets and don't go home. Remember what I said about the railway?"

Still crying, I nodded as I recalled the time we had looked down the embankment at the back of the school and we had seen a passing train. Goose had said that that train might be passing his house, since the railway we could see was joined to the one that went over the Saltmarket and down to the bridge over the river.

"Right then. Get yourself down that embankment and follow the tracks till you reach my house. Tell my ma and da what's happened and they'll make sure that you're all right."

As he said this he wrapped his good arm around my neck and touched his head to mine before, once more, ordering me to "get the fuck out of here".

Finding my way to the embankment was doubly difficult due to the darkness and the tears which were still blinding me but, eventually, I found myself sliding down the rough ground on my arse until I reached the tracks. I turned left and started following the line of the railway, the rails of which were easily distinguishable in the light of the half-moon. I had only travelled about a hundred yards when I heard the sound of a train approaching from the direction I had come. I ducked into the shadow of a large tree as the train passed and slowed to a stop about four hundred yards ahead of me. As I cowered below the tree, I heard the lowing sound of a good number of cows and men's voices urging them off the train. About fifteen minutes later, the train moved off and I was able to continue on my way. I reached the small station, Bellgrove, where the train had stopped and I could see lots of cattle, sheep and pigs packed into pens on the left hand side of the track. I made my way past them as quietly as possible until I reached the bottom of a large, cobbled ramp. I assumed that this must be where the animals would be driven in the morning and I judged, correctly, that I must be passing behind the slaughterhouse where Goose's uncle Peter worked. Thinking of this brought back my feelings of guilt at my abandoning of my pal. I continued to make my way along the railway, interrupted by passing trains and my frequent falls on the uneven surfaces.

Chapter Thirty One

River of no Return

God knows what I must have looked like, covered as I was in the dirt and scrapes I had picked up and McNaughton's blood, which was now beginning to harden on my skin and clothes, when I finally reached the Saltmarket, climbed on to the parapet and tapped on the Laverys' window. It was only after the third series of taps that a light appeared inside the house and the window was opened by Goose's father.

"Mr Lavery, it's me, Willie McCart."

"What the...what's happened, where's Goose?" he stammered as he helped me over from the parapet, through the window and into the house. I started to blurt out what had happened when I noticed that Mrs Lavery was sitting up in bed. I tried to lower my voice to a whisper as I did not want to talk about what Goose had done while his mother was listening.

"Willie McCart," Mrs Lavery almost shouted, her voice both angry and anxious, "just you tell us what has happened to you and is our boy all right."

Forgetting all niceties, I told them the full story and, as I reached the part where I left Goose, I broke down completely.

"I didn't want to leave him, honest to God. He's my pal and I didn't want to leave him, but he said that if I didn't then we would both hang. You know I didn't want to leave him don't you?" I asked them, my voice breaking as I pleaded with them.

"There, there, son" said Mrs Lavery, who had got out of bed and was now holding me to her chest. "We know you didn't want to leave him and if it hadn't been for you he might have been murdered."

As she released me, Mr Lavery also hugged me and, as he did so, I could feel his body trembling.

"I'll tell you something. If Willie hasn't done that bastard in then somebody else *will*. Nobody does that to one of mine and gets away with it. I'll fucking teach him to mess about with my boy."

I looked up as he spoke and I could see his anger-etched face covered in tears. Mrs Lavery tried to soothe him, but he was having none of it and he continued to detail the various forms of retribution that he would visit on McNaughton, if he were to survive and fall into his clutches. Eventually, he calmed down a little when Annie, who had been awakened by the noise from her parents' room came in and asked what was happening. Her mother assured her that everything was all right and took her back into her room. When they had gone, Mr Lavery sat me down and told me to take all of my clothes off. When I had done so he put everything except my boots into the fire. He then scrubbed all of McNaughton's blood from my skin and cleaned up the cuts I had sustained during my escape along the railway. He called through to his wife and asked her to pick out some clothes for me and to make sure that she found some long trousers which would help to make me look older.

"Now listen carefully, Willie. Goose was right when he said that you might be accused of planning the whole thing and if you were found guilty you would both be hung. But they'll still be after you just the same. I know you both gave false names but, if a murder's involved, they'll try everything to track you down. They'll know where you and Goose were first picked up and it will only take a few shillings for tongues to be loosened and for your real identities to be given up. I'm going to have to get you out of Glasgow and as far away as possible and we've not got much time. Once I get you ready, I'll take you round and you can say goodbye to your granny. After that I'll take you to see your ma but that will have to be the last you see of them for a long time and, if that bastard dies, you might never be able to come back at all."

After I was dressed, Mrs Lavery warmed up some soup that she had in a pot and I ate it along with some bread. She kissed me before I left and warned me to be careful. Mr Lavery kept to the shadows as he led me to my grandmother's in Back Wynd. His first knock on the door roused Wolfe and his barking awakened my grandmother and, probably, half the neighbours. When she opened the door, we went in quickly so that we would not be seen. At first, my grandmother was confused, but when Wolfe jumped up into my arms she recognised me immediately, although it took her a little longer to recognise Mr Lavery. Before she could ask any questions or say anything, Mr Lavery gave her a brief account of my predicament, which consisted mainly of my attempt to save my pal. He told her that I would have to leave the city right away and that he was going to arrange this after I had been to see my mother in New Street.

"But, Willie, your ma doesn't live there anymore. That Declan threw her out two weeks ago and I haven't seen her since. I don't know where she is now."

"That can't be helped. Don't you worry, Willie. Once I've got you safely away I'll try and find your ma and make sure she's all right. I'm sorry, but we can't waste time looking for her."

I didn't argue with him, not only because I was growing more afraid as the urgency of my escape gained ever more importance, but also because I was convinced that my mother would probably be in no fit state to offer comfort or encouragement. As we were about to leave, my grandmother stopped us and told me to get my pouch from her sewing box. In all the haste, I had never given my money a second thought. I retrieved the pouch, kissed my grandmother goodbye and left while she held on to Wolfe, who was trying to follow me. When we were outside, I offered the pouch to Mr Lavery in case he needed more money to pay for me to get away.

"You hold on to your money, son. If things work out right, it won't cost anything for you to get away. You better take this as well," he added as he handed me another pouch that he had taken from his jacket pocket. "There's five pounds in silver in there. Keep it safe inside your trousers along with your other money. If you need to buy anything, take out the money when no-one can see you and only take out what you think you'll need."

We left Back Wynd, crossed over the Trongate and started to walk up the High Street in the direction of the Royal Infirmary. Just after we crossed Duke Street, Mr Lavery led me into a close and up two flights of stairs. When we reached the second landing, he knocked on the door on the right hand side. The door was opened after his second knock and there stood Waxy Mulligan peering into the gloom of the gaslight.

"Oh it's yourself Ben. What are you doing up here at this time of night and who's this with you?"

"It's young Willie McCart and he's in trouble. Can we come in for a minute?"

Waxy ushered us both in and Mr Lavery gave him a full account of what had happened. Waxy's curses and threats were almost as extreme as Mr Lavery's had been earlier and it was some time before he settled down sufficiently for Mr Lavery to explain his plan for my escape. They agreed that I would have to hide somewhere with a large population and since it couldn't be in Glasgow then I would have to go to Edinburgh or down to England. Since my accent would have made me stand out like a sore thumb amongst the English, it was decided that Edinburgh would be the safest bet. Mr Lavery was sure that his brother-in-law Duncan would hide me on his canal boat and take me along the Forth and Clyde Canal on his next journey across to Grangemouth. He would be able to arrange for me to transfer to a boat on the Union Canal, which would take me into the heart of Edinburgh. The two men also agreed that I should stay in Waxy's house during the day so that Mr Lavery could go and find out where Duncan was. In addition, I was told to call myself McCartney rather than McCart and to pass myself off as a Protestant, at least until I was safe in Edinburgh. As the dawn was now breaking, Mr Lavery left me with Waxy and made his way further up the High Street towards Port Dundas.

Waxy, who lived on his own, made some breakfast and encouraged me to retell what had happened at Slatefield while we sat together eating. He grew angry again and said that he hoped that I hadn't killed McNaughton not only so that I would avoid the hangman but also so that he and Mr Lavery could get their hands on him. Before he left to open up his shebeen for the day, Waxy told me that I looked dog-tired and that I could get into his bed and catch up with some sleep. I accepted his suggestion, gratefully, and I was sound asleep within minutes of his leaving me on my own.

It was late afternoon when I found myself being awakened by a gentle shake on my shoulder. I opened my eyes and saw that Mr Lavery had returned. He told me that he had managed to find Duncan up at Port Dundas where he had delivered a load of coal and was now loading up his boat with pottery which was to be carried to Grangemouth for export abroad and that he would be leaving first thing the next morning. Duncan had also said that he had a lot of friends on the Union Canal and that he would get one of them to carry me into Edinburgh. When darkness fell, we prepared to leave. Before we left the house, Mr Lavery took a piece of paper out of his pocket and handed it to me saying that he had got it from Waxy. On it was written Father Flynn, St Patricks and other words in a language that Mr Lavery told me was Irish.

"When you get to Edinburgh, make your way to St Patrick's chapel in the Cowgate and ask for Father Flynn. Give him this piece of paper and he'll ask you what your favourite flower is. When he asks you, just show him this and he'll make sure you're safe." As he said this he handed me one of the green rosettes that I had seen him and the other Ribbonmen wearing at my grandfather's funeral.

As we made our way towards Port Dundas, Mr Lavery told me that Duncan didn't want to know why I was running away from Glasgow and that, if asked by anyone else, I was to say that I was only trying to get to Edinburgh to visit my sick mother and that I couldn't afford to pay for a coach or a train. He also told me that he hadn't heard anything about a killing at Slatefield. Normally, news of a killing in the city would spread like wildfire. In his opinion, either McNaughton hadn't died or the authorities were trying to avoid a scandal. Either way, I still had to get out of the city.

It was almost night when we arrived at Duncan's boat. He and his family welcomed us aboard and gave us some food and some strong tea. When the time came for Mr Lavery to leave, I climbed over to the quayside with him. Before I could thank him for all he had done for me, he grasped my right hand and gave it a tight squeeze.

"Willie, in case we should never meet again, I want you to know I am as proud of you as if you were my own son. I also want you to know that I appreciate that the only reason you are having to leave your home and your family is because you tried to save my boy and, for that, me and his ma will be eternally grateful. Cheerio, son and look after yourself now." As he finished speaking, he turned swiftly around and started walking at a brisk pace across the quayside. I stood and watched him fading into the darkness before climbing back aboard the boat.

At first light the following morning, the lines were cast off and the boat slowly steamed away from the quayside. It took us quite a long time to negotiate the winding course of the canal, past the foundries, distilleries, sawmills and flour mills and to reach the junction at Wyndford where Duncan steered his boat to the right branch of the canal and we steamed eastwards. I was standing beside Duncan as we passed the two large lochs at Possil and he informed me that we were now leaving Glasgow. I turned around and looked at the belching factory chimneys and the greyness of the buildings, cowering beneath the weight of the various layers of smoke and wondered, silently, if this would be my last-ever glimpse of the city which had been my birthplace and my home and if I would ever see my friends, especially Goose, for whom I said a silent prayer, or my family again.

Printed in Great Britain
by Amazon

63187591R00149